"How dare you?"

Sophie's voice quivered with rage.

"How dare I bring up the past?" Reed snapped. He pulled her around to face him.

Her little cry had nothing to do with pain and everything to do with the sudden assault of memories. He'd done the very same thing the first time he'd kissed her years ago. She looked up at him, wondering if he remembered, too.

The expression in Reed's eyes was all the answer she needed. For the span of a few heartbeats, it might have been that summer long ago. She could feel his body heat. Heat that was creeping through her like a prairie fire hungrily licking up her defenses.

And, foolish as it was, Sophie waited to see what Reed might do next.

Waited…for some sign of his love.

Dear Reader,

As the air begins to chill outside, curl up under a warm blanket with a mug of hot chocolate and these six fabulous Special Edition novels....

First up is bestselling author Lindsay McKenna's *A Man Alone,* part of her compelling and highly emotional MORGAN'S MERCENARIES: MAVERICK HEARTS series. Meet Captain Thane Hamilton, a wounded Marine who'd closed off his heart long ago, and Paige Black, a woman whose tender loving care may be just what the doctor ordered.

Two new miniseries are launching this month and you're not going to want to miss either one! Look for *The Rancher Next Door,* the first of rising star Susan Mallery's brand-new miniseries, LONE STAR CANYON. Not even a long-standing family feud can prevent love from happening! Also, veteran author Penny Richards pens a juicy and scandalous love story with *Sophie's Scandal,* the first of her wonderful new trilogy—RUMOR HAS IT... that two high school sweethearts are about to recapture the love they once shared....

Next, Jennifer Mikels delivers a wonderfully heartwarming romance between a runaway heiress and a local sheriff with *The Bridal Quest,* the second book in the HERE COME THE BRIDES series. And Diana Whitney brings back her popular STORK EXPRESS series. Could a *Baby of Convenience* be just the thing to bring two unlikely people together?

And last, but not least, please welcome newcomer Tori Carrington to the line. *Just Eight Months Old...* and she'd stolen the hearts of two independent bounty hunters—who just might make the perfect family!

Enjoy these delightful tales, and come back next month for more emotional stories about life, love and family!

Best,
Karen Taylor Richman
Senior Editor

Please address questions and book requests to:
Silhouette Reader Service
U.S.: 3010 Walden Ave., P.O. Box 1325, Buffalo, NY 14269
Canadian: P.O. Box 609, Fort Erie, Ont. L2A 5X3

Sophie's Scandal

PENNY RICHARDS

SPECIAL EDITION™

Published by Silhouette Books

America's Publisher of Contemporary Romance

SILHOUETTE BOOKS

ISBN 0-373-24359-6

SOPHIE'S SCANDAL

This edition published by arrangement with Harlequin Books S.A.

® and TM are trademarks of Harlequin Books S.A., used under license.
Trademarks indicated with ® are registered in the United States Patent
and Trademark Office, the Canadian Trade Marks Office and in other
countries.

Visit Silhouette at www.eHarlequin.com

Printed in U.S.A.

Books by Penny Richards

Silhouette Special Edition

The Greatest Gift of All #921
Where Dreams Have Been #949
Sisters #1015
*The Ranger and the Schoolmarm #1136
*Wildcatter's Kid #1155
Their Child #1213
The No-Nonsense Nanny #1279
†Sophie's Scandal #1359

*Switched at Birth
†Rumor Has It…

Previously published under the pseudonym Bay Matthews

Silhouette Special Edition

Bittersweet Sacrifice #298
Roses and Regrets #347
Some Warm Hunger #391
Lessons in Loving #420
Amarillo by Morning #464
Summer's Promise #505
Laughter on the Wind #613
Sweet Lies, Satin Sighs #648
Worth Waiting For #825
Hardhearted #859

Silhouette Books

Silhouette Christmas Stories 1989
"A Christmas Carole"

PENNY RICHARDS

has also written under the pseudonym Bay Matthews and has been writing for Silhouette for sixteen years. She's been a cosmetologist, an award-winning artist and worked briefly as an interior decorator. She also served a short stint as a short-order cook in her daughter-in-law's café. She has three children and nine grandchildren and lives in Arkansas with her husband of thirty-six years in a soon-to-be-one-hundred-year-old Queen Anne house listed on the National Register of Historic Places. Always behind, she dreams of simplifying her life. Unfortunately, another deadline looms and there is paper to be hung and baseboards to refinish....

MISSOURI

Springfield

Lewiston

Fayetteville

Fort Smith

OKLAHOMA

TENNESSEE

Little Rock

★

Mississippi
River

ARKANSAS

MISSISSIPPI

TEXAS

LOUISIANA

All underlined places
are fictitious.

Prologue

1983

Reality returned in increments of sensation. Reed heard Sophie's sobbing first, over the quieting thrum of his heartbeats and the blaring of Michael Jackson from the car's radio. He became aware of the warmth next, of her breasts, bared by her opened blouse beneath his naked chest, her flesh and his bonded in the most intimate of ways.

He raised his head to look at her. Her eyelashes, drenched with tears, lay in wet crescents against the paleness of her cheeks that bore a splash of honey-hued freckles. Tears trickled down her temples, saturating her strawberry-blond hair. He sucked in a deep breath and smelled the scent of the cheap perfume she wore, a not-so-subtle reminder of the differences in their backgrounds.

Condemned by her tears, Reed moved away from the body that had received him with such fierce abandon and staggered out of the car. Feeling a sickness of the soul he didn't fully understand, he straightened his clothes and sneaked a peek at her.

She hadn't moved. Embarrassed now by the sight of her seminudity, he turned away. They'd been so hot for each other they hadn't even undressed, just pushed and pulled and moved clothing so that they could bare enough flesh to ease their mutual aches. Fighting a feeling of disgust and self-loathing, he stumbled to the rear of the car and filled his lungs with the clean scents of honeysuckle and jessamine.

Nervously, he slid his tongue over his lip. His thoughts were as bitter as the perfume clinging to his mouth. They'd lied. All of them. Every guy at school who'd ever dated Sophie Delaney was nothing but a liar. She didn't sleep around, and she wasn't easy, even though she'd given in to him easily enough. Sophie Delaney had been a virgin. And she'd said she *loved* him.

You told her you loved her, too.

That was different. All guys said the words to get what they wanted. Girls expected it. It was part of the game. But just because the words were said, didn't mean they were meant. He liked Sophie well enough, liked her a lot, in fact. She was sweet and shy and, despite her background, had an air of gentility about her. More important, her interest in him was as real as the diamond in the ring he'd received for his birthday. No one could fake the interest he saw on her face when they talked. It had been her complete absorption that had made him open up to her about his rocky relationship with his father.

She understood him—the things he liked, hated, aspired to—and he liked being with her because she made him feel special. Though she was shy and vulnerable, he sensed an inherent strength about her. When he was with her, encouraged by her to stand up to his dad, he felt invincible. Relying on her courage and basking in her attention could become addictive, but he didn't think that was love. This was just their third date. He hardly knew her. Besides, loving someone meant commitment, and committing to anyone wasn't something he was ready to do. At least not anytime soon. He was too young, and there was too much life he wanted to experience, too many tempting girls to sample.

He'd be a little choosier next time. No more virgins. The thrill of being first wasn't worth the guilt. Jeez, the only reason he and Wes had asked Sophie and her cousin out in the first place was because of their reputations.

Reed cast another glance into the back seat. She was still crying, but thankfully she was sitting up and had pulled her skirt back down. Her blouse was still open, and the front clasp of her bra was still undone. He tried not to stare. Sensing his scrutiny, she turned to look at him, her tear-drenched eyes filled with…what? Remorse? Pleading?

Reed turned away from her and stuffed his shirt into his jeans. A fresh round of crying punctuated the stillness of the summer evening. It was too early to take her home, but the expression in her eyes only increased his guilt, and he couldn't handle much more of that.

He felt her hand on his shoulder and jerked away from her touch as if it were hot. Turning, he saw the sheen of tears in her eyes. She hadn't bothered to button her blouse.

"You're sorry it happened, aren't you?"

"No!" he lied, forcing himself to meet the condemnation in her eyes.

She took his hand and pressed it to the fullness of her breast. Reed closed his eyes and gritted his teeth. Her skin was like warm silk.

"Yes, you are. I thought you'd be happy you were the first, that I hadn't slept with all those boys who told you I had."

His eyes flew open, and he pulled his hand free. "I am." That much, at least, was true. Though he didn't understand why, a part of him was glad her reputation was undeserved.

She choked back a sob. "Then why are you pushing me away?"

"I'm sorry," he said, shrugging. "I didn't mean to."

She stared at him for a long time, then hooked her bra and began to do up her buttons. "Maybe you should take me home."

Reed couldn't stifle the relief that surged through him. "Sure. If that's what you want."

"What I want is to spend some time with you. But I have a feeling you want to get rid of me."

"That's not true!" But they both knew he was protesting too much.

"I thought you felt something for me," she said, her voice trembling, her pain obvious. "I guess I was wrong. Was I just another girl to you, Reed? Another conquest?"

"No." If it had started out that way, it certainly wasn't how he felt now. Conquests brought about pride and a feeling of victory. He felt nothing but a crushing, unbearable guilt. He met the condemnation in her eyes. "No. You aren't that."

"Then what am I, Reed?" she asked. Suddenly she looked far older than her sixteen years. Seemed older.

"I don't know, Sophie, and that's the truth."

Her teeth came down on her bottom lip, and she nodded. Then, with a detachment he envied, she rounded the rear of the car. After a moment he followed her. He drove her home, stopping at the end of the lane. She'd refused to let him pick her up at her house.

She slipped out of the Firebird and leaned down to look at him. "I love you."

"I love you, too," he said, knowing as he said it he had no idea what his feelings were.

"Call me?"

"Sure. Soon."

The look in her eyes had told him she knew he was lying. "No matter what happens, Reed, I want you to know that I don't have any regrets. I'm glad it was you. And I'll never be sorry it happened."

It was a statement they would both think about often in the next seventeen years.

Chapter One

"I want to go home, Sophe. I want my life back, such as it may be. And I want you to go with me."

Filled with a fresh rush of the guilty anguish that seldom left her, Sophie Carlisle met the earnest entreaty in her brother's dark-blue eyes and felt the hot welling of tears in her own. After all he'd done for her, after literally giving up a chunk of his life for her, how could she deny him anything? Except for this…this plea to go back to the place where the two of them had grown up and confront the past she'd worked so hard at forgetting, she couldn't.

Yet, even with the certainty that going back to Lewiston, Arkansas, for any length of time held the potential for destruction, she couldn't stifle the sudden, violent and unexpected yearning to see Reed Hardisty again. As she had so often in the past, she suppressed the longing. There lay heartbreak and humiliation, not to mention untold suffering and death.

"I'm sorry." The words were a distressed whisper. "You won't go?"

Sophie shook her head. "I won't go, and I'm sorry my actions robbed you of so much of your life."

Donovan leaped to his feet and rounded the antique table sitting on the polished hardwood floor of the kitchen of Sophie's Baton Rouge condo. He grabbed her shoulders and hauled her to her feet.

"Stop it!" he said, giving her a hard shake, the way he had when they were kids and he wanted to impress something on her. Then, as if realizing what he was doing, he stopped and pushed her strawberry-blond hair away from her face, his calloused fingers gentle as they swiped baby-fine strands from her cheek and tucked them behind her ear.

"We've been through this a hundred times. So you shot the sorry bastard who donated the sperm for our conception. If you hadn't, he'd probably have killed you, and you know it."

Donovan was right. If she hadn't protected herself from her father's flying fists seventeen years ago, she'd have been the one left on the floor, dead. There was little doubt in her mind that her dad—difficult even when he wasn't drinking and meaner than Satan when he was—would have finished what he'd started the previous week when he'd left her with a cracked rib and a blackened eye, not to mention other various and sundry bruises.

But knowing that what she'd done, she'd done to save her own life and the life of the baby she'd been carrying didn't change the fact that she'd taken a life or lessen the constant guilt she felt for letting her brother take the blame for what she'd done.

"Maybe he would have killed me, but you're the one who paid with several years of your life, while I walked away scot-free."

"Like hell," Donovan said, releasing his hold on her and drawing her into a comforting embrace. "You've suffered as much as I have. The only difference is that I was behind bars."

Sophie clung to him, battling her tears and drawing strength from the kind of hard-hewn muscle and sinew that had been purchased with hours of hard work instead of at a posh fitness center. He was right. She'd lived in a prison of her own making. After he'd told the authorities that he was the one who'd pulled the trigger that night, there hadn't been a day she hadn't agonized over the events that had taken place, not a night that had passed that she hadn't hated herself for the weakness that had let him make such a sacrifice for her. And even though he'd been free for years, Sophie was still bound by the memory of her actions and the consequences of her weakness.

"Why do you want to go back?" she asked now, trying to make sense out of his sudden urge to go back to a place where people had looked down on them both for no other reason than that they'd been unfortunate enough to be sired by Hutch Delaney.

She felt Donovan stiffen and knew she'd inadvertently touched some sort of exposed nerve. Frowning and pulling back, she said, "Donovan?"

He met her questioning gaze with a steady calm. "I have some unfinished business there."

Sophie's confusion deepened. "You were twenty

years old when you left. What possible kind of unfinished business could you have left behind?''

Donovan smiled, the roguish, devil-may-care smile that never failed to set feminine hearts aflutter. ''Are you poking that pretty nose into my business, little sister? Or are you playin' shrink?''

''I'm just curious as to why you'd want to subject yourself to what's bound to happen if you go back.''

''What'll happen, Sophe? Will people whisper behind my back about the bad thing they think I did?'' He lifted wide shoulders in a shrug. ''They talked before. Will they try to steer their virtuous daughters out of harm's way? Well, all the girls I might have been interested in are all grown-up now, able to make decisions without daddy and mama's input.''

Though there was a light tone to his voice, Sophie noticed the tightening of his lips. Understanding hit her with the force of a gale wind. She sucked in a sharp breath. ''This is about a woman, isn't it?''

''What?'' he asked with a guileless expression.

Sophie's head made a slow side-to-side movement. ''This sudden urge to go back.''

''No!'' Donovan said, the edge in his voice unmistakable.

The fact that he turned away and wouldn't meet her gaze was a dead giveaway that she'd scored a direct hit. Grabbing his chambray shirtsleeve, she dragged him around to face her. ''Who is she?''

''No one,'' he insisted. ''It's just that the probate has been satisfied on Mama's place, which you'd know if you read the letters Reed sends instead of sticking them in the drawer. It's ours free and clear, and I might as well make use of it—if you don't want it.''

Sophie's face blanched. "You actually think I might want to live in that house? Never! And I can't believe you would, either."

"There's nothing there that can hurt us but memories, Sophe, and we've both got those no matter where we are. I'm pushing forty. I want some roots. Something of my own. I have some ideas for renovating the house, and I'm pretty handy with a hammer and saw. You won't recognize the place when I'm finished."

"Why would you want to move away? You have a wonderful job here."

"Right," Donovan said, a hint of disgust in his voice. "A job. Most of the work Art Leonard gets is because I've built a reputation for his company. I'm tired of making big bucks for someone else. It's my turn."

"And you think you're going to make big bucks as a landscape architect in Lewiston?"

"No, but I can make a decent living doing what I like to do and being my own boss. I know a lot of people in the business, and I think that with almost thirty acres at my disposal and a lot more cutover timber land out there that can be bought at a reasonable price, I can satisfy the need of the locals and maybe specialize in growing something to market to some of the big-time guys, like Art Leonard. Of course, I'll buy out your half of the place, if you want to sell," he added.

"If you're serious about this wild scheme, you can *have* my half," Sophie said, shaking her head and plopping back down in her seat.

"I'm dead serious, but—"

Knowing he was about to object to her offer, she

held up a silencing hand. "This is *not* up for discussion. Good Lord, Donovan, it's the least I can do to help you make a fresh start."

"How about making one with me?"

Incredulity gleamed in her eyes, and she uttered a short, bitter laugh. "Go back to Lewiston and open up a family counseling clinic? I'd starve to death."

"That's funny," he said, a contemplative gleam in his eyes. "I never knew you did it for the money."

"I don't," she snapped.

Donovan grinned. "I know. I also know that you, better than anyone, should know there are people who need help no matter how small the town. And you certainly wouldn't starve. You wouldn't pull down what you're bringing in now, but you'd do okay. Besides, I know Jake left you pretty well fixed, even if you never worked again."

"That has nothing to do with anything. I have a life here. Friends."

"Yeah?" he said with a cocked eyebrow. "Name one."

Sophie started to spout a name, then realized that the woman was more an acquaintance than a real friend, as was every other person whose name popped into her mind. She had never found it easy to establish close relationships. The friends she and Jake had cultivated during their marriage had been mostly the wives of his business colleagues, other investment bankers. Jake had played golf with his buddies and infrequently, Sophie now realized, she had held dinners in their home. But when Jake had died, so had the friendships. When she'd repeatedly declined the invitations that had come her way, they'd stopped coming. Until now she hadn't even noticed.

"I'm not a very social person," she said in her own defense.

"That's the understatement of the century."

"I'm just—" she shrugged "—happy with you, Cass and my life here."

"Are you?" he asked, his blue gaze probing hers.

"What's that supposed to mean?"

"Are you really happy, or just content to let things go on as they are as long as nothing comes along to disturb your quiet little life?"

She opened her mouth to tell him that she was really happy, but for some reason she couldn't find those words any easier than she'd been able to find the names of the women she'd considered her friends.

"Can't say it, huh?" Donovan taunted in a gentle voice. "And I'm leaving. It'll just be you and Cass."

"You're really doing this?" she asked, disbelief echoing in her voice.

"I've already given two weeks' notice."

Filled with a sudden emptiness, Sophie nodded. She rubbed her palms down the thighs of her worn jeans and exhaled a deep sigh. "Well, then. There's nothing else I can say, is there?"

"Say you and Cass will come with me. Just for two weeks. I know you have some vacation time planned out. I even know it starts two weeks from now."

Sophie glanced sharply at him. "How do you know that?"

"Gracie told me. You know that all I have to do is smile at her, and she's putty in my hands."

Sophie couldn't help her own smile. Gracie Morris was middle-aged, married and had ten grandchildren, but she did indeed have a soft spot for Donovan.

"I've made plans for Cassidy and me to go to the Keys."

"I canceled them."

"You what!"

"Not really," he said, relenting. "But *you* could. People do it all the time."

Exasperated with him, with the whole conversation, Sophie shook her head. "You're incorrigible."

"If that means desperate, then you're right."

She pinned him with a steely look. "You know perfectly well what incorrigible means."

"C'mon, sis," he wheedled. "Just come and help get me set up. I need someone to drive the Explorer while I drive the U-Haul and pull the truck, not to mention that someone will need to help me get all my stuff put where it belongs. Otherwise I might put my underwear in the dish towel drawer."

"Is this pitiful speech supposed to sway me, Mr. Organization Personified?"

"I was hoping it would."

She sighed again. Abandoning all hope of talking him out of the crazy notion, and sensing the inherent danger for them all, she said, "Let me think about it. This whole thing has hit me pretty hard."

Donovan, too, became suddenly serious. He took her cold hands in his. "I know," he told her, "but I didn't want to tell you until I had everything set to go."

"Are you sure this is what you want to do?"

"Positive." There was no doubt in his eyes. "I've saved some money, and thanks to Jake's guidance, it's bringing in more. I'm not rich, but I've got enough to carry me through for a while."

"Okay," she said. "Just tell me one thing."

He nodded. "Anything."

She gave him a mischievous grin. "Who's the woman?"

The disbelief in his eyes was comical. It wasn't often that Sophie was able to turn the tables on her big brother. For a second or two she thought he might renege, but then he gave a small shrug of resignation and tossed out the name without the slightest bit of animosity.

"Lara Hardisty."

If he'd said the queen mother, Sophie couldn't have been more shocked. "Lara Hardisty? I didn't even know you knew Lara Hardisty."

"Of course I know her. I used to do yard work for them, remember?"

"I remember, but—"

"I mowed the place for five summers," Donovan told her, his gaze focussed on someplace in the distant past. "I watched her grow up. And I fell in love with her."

"But Donovan, she's—"

He turned to look at her. "What? The banker's daughter? Above me? Reed's ex-wife?" His smile was grim. "Don't I know it. She did, too, but she loved me, anyway. Can you believe it?"

"Of course I can believe it. Being your sister and knowing you the way I do, I see all your good qualities. But Lara Hardisty! She's so...I don't know...sophisticated and classy."

Donovan laughed, but there was no rancor in the sound. "Meaning I'm not."

"Meaning you clean up very nicely, thank you, and you have excellent taste in clothing and everything

else as well as a love for the arts, but back then..."
She broke off with a shrug.

"I know. Back then all I did was clean up pretty good," he said with a smile. "I was just Hutch Delaney's boy, who'd been taught manners and respect by a woman who'd learned all she knew about those qualities from *her* employer."

"Isabelle Duncan," Sophie said, a vision of the woman surfacing as it had several times in the past six months.

Ruby Delaney had cleaned house and cooked for Isabelle for thirty years—since Sophie was three. Donovan had done her yard work, garnering his basic horticultural knowledge from her. The now seventy-something woman had been one of the handful of mourners who'd attended Ruby Delaney's funeral seven months ago, even attending the graveside service some twenty miles out in the country.

"She was good to Mama."

"Yeah, she was," Donovan agreed. "She's a good woman. She told me she'd buy the place if we wanted to sell, or if I ever wanted to come back and needed anything, to give her a call."

Sophie glanced at him. "She did?"

He smiled. "I think when I realized that not everyone in Lewiston looked on me like I was some dangerous criminal, is when I got the idea to move back," he confided. "For better or worse, that's home to me, Sophe."

Sophie grasped his meaning better than he might think. If home was where the heart was, and Donovan's heart was still with Lara Hardisty, his feelings made perfect sense. It was a concept Sophie understood, because as much as she hated to admit it, a part of her heart would always belong to the man who'd fathered her daughter.

"I've spoken with Isabelle several times the past few weeks," Donovan said. "She thinks I have a workable idea and told me to get a business and marketing plan together to present to the bank, which I did. She still carries a lot of clout with the board." He grinned again. "With Isabelle Duncan on my side, how can I go wrong? C'mon, Sophe. Just for a couple of weeks."

Sophie looked into her brother's pleading eyes. Her plans for the Keys were easily canceled. She and Cassidy had been there the year before, so it wasn't as if nixing the trip would deprive Cass of an opportunity she might never have again. Sophie sighed. She was weakening and she knew it.

"I'll think about it," she said again, her voice sharper than she intended.

Donovan smiled, seeing something in her eyes, hearing it in her voice and knowing somehow that he'd already been granted his wish.

When her brother left, Sophie went to the sink to fill the teakettle for a cup of Darjeeling. Darn Donovan's hide! she thought, as she set the delicate, violet chintz cup and saucer on the table. He knew which buttons to push. He always had. Knowing he was her closest adult friend since Jake died, he'd played on her sympathy by asking her to come and help him get settled, a challenge he'd known she couldn't deny. She was too much like their mother in that respect.

So go help him get settled, then come back. No big deal, right?

Wrong. Going back was always a big deal. When

she'd made the infrequent trips back home before her mother died, the combined anticipation and dread at the possibility of seeing Reed began wearing on her nerves long before she left. She was always careful to spend most of her time at the house—as painful as that was—and when that wasn't possible, she'd gone out of her way to stay clear of the places Reed might frequent. Never once during the past seventeen years had she run into him. Surely she could manage it one more time. But then, she'd never stayed two weeks before.

Sophie chewed on a nail, a habit she reverted to when she was under stress. Was she insane or just a masochist to even consider Donovan's suggestion? And what about Cassidy? There was always the remote possibility that she might find out the truth.

You're being paranoid, Sophia Carlisle. Who's going to tell her—Reed?

With the deaths of her parents and Jake, few people knew the truth of Cassidy's paternity, and Sophie doubted that Reed and his father would admit to it. In fact, there was no reason to be so concerned. Reed had no doubt been thrilled when he found out she'd married someone else as soon as she'd left town.

Reed. Why did thinking of him still have the power to hurt her after all these years, especially since she'd known when she'd gone out with him that nothing could come of it? Why had she felt that sense of betrayal when she remembered the things her father had told her after he'd confronted Reed and his father about her pregnancy: Reed, son of the town's leading physician, wanted no part of her or her baby, something proved by the fact that his father had handed over enough money so Sophie could leave town, have an abortion, getting rid of Reed's mistake, and start a new life.

A sudden chill swept through Sophie. Thank God, she'd never once considered the abortion. To imagine life without Cassidy was to envision a life without sunlight. All the mental anguish and the physical hardships had been worth it. And even if her sixteen-year-old daughter sometimes became hard to handle as her rampaging hormones played havoc with her usually sunny disposition, Sophie would never have traded her life with Cassidy for a life without her.

Sophie had taken a round of abuse when Hutch had first heard of her condition. She had been afraid that one of the body blows he favored would make her lose Reed's baby. Hutch had even broken one of his own rules that night. He'd hit her in the face, something he avoided at all costs—at least with her and her mother. After all, split lips and black eyes were hard for a woman to explain away. Donovan was another matter. He'd gained the reputation for being a brawler, a fabrication he'd set up to cover his own battle scars.

Thankfully, like an avenging angel, Donovan had come through the door and stepped between her and their father. Hutch, whose size and meanness stacked the odds in his favor against Donovan's youth and agility, had beaten Donovan until Sophie and Ruby had both begged him to stop before he killed him. Donovan had said he'd kill Hutch if he laid another hand on any one of them.

A week later, Hutch had done just that, and it had been Sophie who'd done the shooting. Donovan had come in seconds after the shotgun discharged and found Hutch lying on the floor. Beneath the pallor of his shock, Donovan's face still bore the week-old marks of Hutch's fists. He had taken in Sophie's bleeding lip and the cut on her cheekbone where the diamond ring Hutch had won in a poker game had left its mark and said, "What happened?"

With her ears still ringing from the blast of the shotgun, Sophie dragged her gaze away from her father's prostrate form. A fresh batch of tears rolled down her cheeks. "He went t-to see Reed and Mr. Hardisty about me being pregnant. He said Reed didn't want any part of me or the baby. Mr. Hardisty gave Daddy the money so I could have an abortion and leave town."

"Hardisty gave him the money?" Donovan said, glancing toward the table where hundred-dollar bills lay spread out like a fan. "A payoff, huh?"

She nodded and her tears began to fall faster. Donovan's lips twisted into a parody of a smile. A bit of color had returned to his face. "And you told him you wouldn't do it."

Sophie wrapped her arms across her middle in a protective gesture. "This is a baby, Donovan. Reed's baby. Even if he doesn't want us, I can't change the way I feel about him, and I can't get rid of the baby just to make his life easier. Or mine, either."

Donovan nodded, turned to look at Hutch for a moment, then turned back to her. He made a wide berth around the their father's bleeding body, crossed the room and took the twelve-gauge shotgun from her. He moved to the place where she'd been standing, and, in a practiced gesture, fitted the shotgun to his shoulder. Then he squinted down the length of the barrel and placed his finger on the trigger.

Outside, an owl hooted loudly. The ticking of the

plastic clock hanging on the kitchen wall kept time with the heavy thudding of Sophie's heart. She drew in a deep breath to steady herself, but the lingering scent of the liver and onions Ruby had left warming in the oven combined with her shock to make her gag.

Choking back the nausea with an effort, she asked, "What are you doing?"

"Listen carefully, Sophe, while I tell you how it happened."

With her body trembling in horror and shock at the magnitude of what she'd done, she said, "I know how it happened."

"Just shut up and listen to me!"

Stunned to silence by the insistence in his voice, Sophie nodded.

"I came home from my date and he was beating you," Donovan said, dropping the firearm onto the floor. "Don't say anything about being pregnant by Reed Hardisty. Say it was because he was drunk and didn't want liver and onions for dinner—anything! I came in and told him to stop, and he made a swipe at me, but he was too drunk, and I stepped out of his reach. Then he started working on you again, and I ran around the two of you, grabbed the shotgun down from the rack. I called out to him, and he turned around. I told him to leave you alone again. He rushed me, I panicked and pulled the trigger."

Sophie could only stare at him in stunned disbelief. "B-but…you didn't shoot him. I did."

Donovan's jaw set in the anger she saw on his face all too often. He took her shoulders in his big, rough hands and shook her, hard. "You do as I tell you!" he gritted. "He's dead, Sophe. If you say you did it, you might have to spend time in jail."

She felt the color leech from her face, felt the starch

leave her bones. If he hadn't been holding on to her, she'd have collapsed. "B-but if you say you did it, *you'll* go to jail."

"Better me than you. Think about the baby, Sophe."

"But—"

"No buts."

He'd headed for the phone, insisting all the while that she do as he said. In the end she'd agreed, too sick and scared to think clearly. As soon as he called the sheriff's department and told them what he'd allegedly done, he'd hung up and called their mother, who was sitting with a sick friend. He'd told her to come home—there'd been an accident—then hung up before she could ask any questions. Then he'd gone to the table and begun counting the money.

"There's five thousand dollars here," he'd told her, pressing the wad of bills into her hands. "Go hide it in the shed somewhere. When all this blows over, take it and get out of here. Start a new life for you and your baby."

"I can't!" she cried, almost as horrified at the thought of leaving everything familiar as she was of going to jail. "We should turn it in. It's not mine."

"Like hell it's not. Reed won't stand up to his responsibility, and his daddy wanted you to have it, so take it. It's the least the high-and-mighty Hardistys can do for you."

"But they'll tell the sheriff."

"No, they won't," Donovan had said. "Rowland Hardisty won't want anyone to know about you and his son. If you did tell the cops and they confronted him, he'd deny it. Be smart, Sophe. Take the money and go."

In the end, with the sirens screaming in the distance, Sophie had done as Donovan begged her to do. When Sheriff Micah Lawrence had asked what happened, Donovan repeated what he'd told her he would say. The sheriff's sharp blue eyes had searched Donovan's with the relentlessness he was rumored to have when it came to getting at the truth.

When he'd pinned that probing stare on Sophie and asked for corroboration of point after point, she'd given it. But with every nod of her head, every whispered "yes," she'd heard the clanging of the jail doors slamming, seen Donovan's capable hands wrap around the bars, visualized his face behind those bars, growing older. It was a memory that had stayed with her, even though he'd been out of prison now for years.

When Ruby Delaney had arrived and seen them carrying a body bag from her house, her frantic gaze had sought the cluster of people in the room, to see who was still standing. To Sophie, the relief on her mother's face that the dead body was neither her daughter's nor son's was clear. But when she was told what had happened, she'd looked from Sophie to Donovan and then to Micah Lawrence. Then she'd buried her face in her hands and begun to sob!

The men in the room had assumed that she'd loved her husband, even though they, and everyone else in town, suspected Hutch used his family for punching bags from time to time. The sheriff had started toward her, as if he might offer her some comfort, but stopped.

Her mother's keening wail had struck Sophie's heart like the point of a sharp instrument. She'd known she couldn't go through with Donovan's scheme. With her gaze clinging to his, she'd opened her mouth to blurt out the truth, but Donovan had taken her in a tight grip and crushed her face against his chest and whispered hoarsely, "Don't."

Once again the law officials had misunderstood. Shortly afterward, they had handcuffed him and taken him to the county jail. When everyone had gone, Sophie and her mother had collapsed into each other's arms and cried for what seemed like, and probably was, hours. Then they'd climbed into Ruby's ancient Ford and driven to Sophie's Aunt Opal's to spend the night.

Isabelle Duncan had offered to pay for Donovan to have someone other than a court-appointed attorney, and Ruby accepted her employer's generous offer with gratitude. Unable to bear the guilt, Sophie told her mother about the money, and Ruby agreed with Donovan: Sophie should take the money and start over somewhere. When, three days after the shooting, Sophie had received a call from Rowland Hardisty that urged her to do the same, she'd found the strength to follow through.

Promising that she would keep the sheriff's department informed of her whereabouts and would be at the trial to testify, she'd given Ruby a thousand dollars and headed to Louisiana. The trial took place some seven months later, and, true to her word, Sophie had come back to tell her side of what happened. To the surprise of the Lewiston citizenry, she'd come back with a husband who was obviously crazy about her and, just as clearly, about to be delivered of a baby.

That news—which was almost as juicy as the murder trial—spread through town on a wave of whispers. It reached the medical offices of Rowland Hardisty. The younger Hardisty heard it from his friend Wes

Grayson, who'd seen Sophie with her cousin, Justine, at the Burger Barn.

Reed Hardisty pretended to be unaffected, but he'd been stunned. While he joked and agreed that she was as easy as her reputation allowed, he was hurting inside, more than he would ever have thought possible. It was only later that anger replaced the pain. He would never know the agony that period of farce had cost Sophie.

The case was cut-and-dried. The facts were laid out, the objective to see that Donovan served as little time as possible. He might have gotten a lighter sentence if one of Hutch's friends hadn't claimed Donovan had threatened to kill his dad. Donovan's lawyer cried "Hearsay," and the prosecution and defense did their usual thrust and parry. Donovan wound up serving more time than he should have, considering the circumstances, but less than he might have.

After Sophie gave birth to Reed Hardisty's daughter, she visited her brother whenever she could. She took her GED and enrolled in the community college in Bossier City. She and Jake worked their schedules around Cassidy and his job. Sometimes, over the years, Ruby had traveled to Louisiana to visit. Even more rarely, Sophie and her family went back to Arkansas for a brief stay. Sometimes they talked about the night Hutch had been killed and how much they missed Donovan. Sophie kept her word to Donovan. She never told her mother that it should have been her behind bars instead of her brother. She didn't have to.

Somehow, she sensed that Ruby knew.

Chapter Two

"Why haven't you turned on the lights?"

The sound of her daughter's voice dragged Sophie from the darkness of her thoughts. She must have sat there for hours, remembering the pain of the past while the late-spring day eased into dusk. She hadn't even heard Cassidy's key in the lock.

"I didn't realize how late it was getting," she said in reply to Cassidy's question.

With her brown hair swinging around her face, Cassidy leaned over and gave Sophie a smacking kiss on the cheek. "You must have been thinking about some pretty heavy stuff."

"I was."

The teasing glint vanished from Cassidy's eyes. "Is anything wrong?"

No, nothing. Your uncle has just announced he's moving away, leaving us alone. But not to worry,

Cass, he wants us to pack up the lives we've built here and go with him. Back to the place where people think we're no better than pond scum. Back to the place where your real father lives.

Sophie and Jake had made it a practice to be as honest as possible with Cassidy about the things that might affect her life. As she'd approached her dating years, they, along with Donovan, had set her down and told her about Hutch's shooting, omitting—at Sophie's insistence and Donovan and Jake's opposition—the part about Reed Hardisty and Sophie's pregnancy. She hadn't been ready to tell Cassidy that Jake wasn't her father, but she was ready to warn her against the dangers of abusive relationships, something so many young girls found themselves involved in.

Sophie knew she had no choice but to tell her daughter what was going on, since Donovan's leaving would have a profound effect on Cassidy's life. "Everything's fine, honey," she said. "But your uncle Donovan dropped a bombshell on me this afternoon."

"Don't tell me he's getting married!" Cassidy asked, her face flushed with happiness. Cassidy adored her uncle and had grown even closer to her him since her father's death. She considered Donovan's bachelorhood a terrible waste. Her greatest desire was to see him happily married with lots of little Donovans running around. Losing him would be hard on her.

"Not that I know of," Sophie said. "Why don't you sit down."

An expression of alarm molded Cassidy's features. "Mom… Oh, gosh, Mom, he isn't dying or anything, is he?"

Since Donovan was the same age as the fathers of some of Cassidy's friends, and one of them had recently suffered a fatal heart attack, her fear was legitimate.

"No! Of course not!"

"Then what is it?"

Sophie plunged in. "He wants to move back to Lewiston, to Grandma's house."

Cassidy's face paled. "Why?"

Sophie's heart ached at the desolation she saw in her daughter's eyes. "Because he wants to be his own boss, and the land and house are ours since Grandma died. He's going to go into the nursery and landscape business."

Cassidy's face bore more sorrow than anger. "But I'll never get to see him."

"We can visit."

"It won't be the same," she wailed.

Cassidy wasn't a child who could be mollified with a few well-chosen words that distorted the reality of the situation. She was a very sharp young woman with more than a fair amount of common sense.

"No," Sophie agreed. "It won't be the same."

Cassidy crossed her arms over her breasts and stomped her sandaled foot in a rare show of pique, something she hadn't done since she was a child. "How can he do this to us?"

"Honey," Sophie said in a gentle tone. "This isn't about us. It's about your uncle and what will make him happy. It's his life, and he deserves to live it the way he wants. Where he wants."

"I suppose," Cassidy said on a sigh. She took a glass from the cabinet, went to the refrigerator and poured herself some orange juice. Then she leaned against the cabinet and regarded Sophie thoughtfully. "It would be fun to go away and do something different. Start a new life."

The statement was spoken with a wistfulness that surprised Sophie. She'd had no idea Cassidy was dissatisfied with their life in Baton Rouge, which she told her.

Cassidy sat down across from Sophie. "I'm not really, like, you know…unhappy. It's just that you've been working so much."

Talons of guilt snagged Sophie's soul. She'd immersed herself in her work since Jake died, taking more patients, staying late so there would be fewer hours at home without him. Suddenly she realized there'd been fewer hours with Cassidy, too. Alarm clamored through her. Dear God! She'd fallen into the same trap she helped so many parents climb out of. She'd been so wrapped up in her own loss, her own misery, she'd emotionally abandoned her only child.

"It's okay, Mom," Cassidy said, seeing the panic on her mother's face. "It didn't warp me or anything, but I've been lonely sometimes."

Sophie got up, crossed the small space and put her arms around her only child, orange juice and all. "Oh, Cass! I'm so sorry. I guess I thought with all your extracurricular activities at school and Barry—"

"Barry and I have been finished for over two weeks, Mom."

Sophie pulled back from Cassidy in disbelief. "You're kidding!"

"No." Cassidy smiled. "Don't tell me you haven't noticed that he isn't calling."

"I did, but I just thought he was on restriction or something."

"Restriction? Mr. Perfect? I don't think so."

"What happened?"

"He said he thought we should break up for the summer. That it wasn't fair for us to be tied to each other, since he's going to Europe and we wouldn't be able to see or talk to each other every day."

"Translate that to he wants to be footloose and fancy-free so he can flirt with the girls he meets."

"That's what I thought," Cassidy said.

Sophie's fingertips caressed her daughter's cheek. "Are you okay with this, honey?"

Cassidy shrugged. "Yeah. I think my pride was more hurt than my heart. I mean, it isn't like I expected us to be together forever."

Sophie regarded her daughter with a thoughtful expression. Cassidy was the same age she'd been when she'd gotten pregnant by Reed Hardisty. For the first time in her life Sophie understood how very young she'd been. How naive to think, or even hope, that Reed would see her for something more than she was or want more from her than he had.

Though she'd been exposed to a lot of ugliness as Hutch Delaney's daughter, in many ways, she'd been an unworldly sixteen, so gullible that when one of the richest boys in town had asked her out she'd gone, so naive that she'd fallen for his "I love you" line. They'd had nothing in common and never would, except a daughter he'd wanted her to get rid of. Thank God Cassidy was more sophisticated and realistic about boy-girl relationships.

"When is he leaving?"

"Who?" Sophie asked, so wrapped up in her

thoughts she'd forgotten what they were talking about.

"Uncle Donovan, of course." Cassidy smiled. "Where were you, Mom?"

"In Lewiston."

"You didn't like living there, did you?"

"It wasn't the place, Cass," Sophie said with a heavy sigh. "Places are neutral. It was the people. We were pretty well considered trash."

"Why? Because you were poor and lived out in the country in an old house? I know it wasn't fancy, but Grandma kept it spotless."

"Yeah, she did. I think mostly it was because of my dad. He drank, and he couldn't hold a job for long. How people perceived him seemed to rub off on all of us."

"That isn't fair!"

"Life isn't—"

"—always fair. I know." Cassidy interrupted. "You didn't answer my question. When is Uncle Donovan leaving?"

"In two weeks." Sophie paused. Considering Cassidy's statement, she was hesitant to tell her Donovan wanted them to move, too. Seeing the sorrow on her daughter's face, she decided to compromise. "He wants us to go help him settle in."

Cassidy's face brightened. "He does? That'd be fun."

Sophie made a mental note to call and cancel their flight to Florida. "Scrubbing and cleaning fun? Since when?"

"I mean being in the country will be fun for a change. Maybe I can help him decide where to put the greenhouses. Do you think he'll start any seedlings? I can help with that. Or is he going to try to—''

''Whoa!'' Sophie said, surprised by Cassidy's enthusiasm. ''Do you actually like getting your hands dirty?''

The question seemed to catch Cassidy off guard. ''Well, since you asked, I guess I do. You remember when Daddy died, how Uncle Donovan took me with him to the greenhouses. He showed me how to do root cuttings and how to start seedlings. Did you know that plants move all the time, even though they seem like they're still?''

''They do?'' Sophie asked.

''Yes.'' Cassidy laughed, her face flushed with pleasure. ''Don't tell him, but I could listen to Uncle Donovan go on about plants forever, and I like watching things grow. It's a miracle that everything that makes a plant what it is at maturity comes from one tiny seed, isn't it?''

Indeed it was, Sophie thought, regarding the enthusiasm on the face of the daughter that had grown from her and Reed's seed. A miracle.

On the very day that Donovan broke the news of his move to Sophie and she passed the information on to Cassidy, the Lewiston grapevine was busily spreading the word of his return.

It was a Tuesday, the day Isabelle Duncan and the other board members of the bank typically met to discuss loan applications. When she presented Donovan's financial statements and his business plan, the room exploded in various stages of outrage and disbelief.

Wes Grayson, Reed Hardisty's law partner and best

friend, who sat on the board because his father, Phil, had once been its president and he held the second most shares, secretly thought Donovan had done the world a favor in ridding it of Hutch Delaney.

A true Southern gentleman in beliefs, if not in looks, Wes believed a woman should be protected and that Donovan should be able to come back if he wanted to, though he was at a loss as to understand why he'd want to. A couple of other board members were willing to give him the benefit of the doubt, but the majority were horrified at the thought of his return, much less lending him money to start a business. Comments like "ex-jailbird," "killer" and "no-good boy of Hutch Delaney's" resounded through the room.

As eccentric as she was, they never dreamed Isabelle would be a problem. If, when they'd lowered Ruby Delaney's body into the raw wound of the earth seven months earlier, Isabelle had looked out of place in her mink coat—which was controversial because it was the real thing as well as because it was four decades out of style—no one would have dared say. Nor would they have said anything about why she didn't get a new car—she could certainly afford it—instead of holding on to the aged Bentley that gleamed in the anemic winter sunlight. No bigger than a minute and richer than God, as Sophie's mother used to say, Isabelle Duncan had always been—and still was—a force to be reckoned with in the county.

She countered the attacks against Donovan with comments dealing with the board's "Christian charity," "self-defense" and "debt to society." Then she'd extolled Donovan's mother's loyalty and honesty during her more than thirty years of keeping house for Isabelle and her dear, departed Leo.

She praised Donovan's work ethic as a young man. She noted his pristine credit, the thought that had gone into—and the professionalism of—his business plan and the feasibility of it for their area. She talked about the dearth of industry in the county, the need for economic growth and jobs for the local citizenry. Then she'd made an outright threat to pull her money out of the bank if they didn't okay the loan.

A collective gasp of surprise mirrored the board's shock. The controlling stockholder, Isabelle had never before flaunted the fact that she could make or break the bank. A shrewd businesswoman and no fool when it came to judging character, they had never seen her so obstinate, so blind to risk. It was clear that her mind was finally starting to go. But no one said the words. Instead, appalled by the threat, dumbfounded by the way she dug in her heels, they voted six to two to give Donovan the money.

With a pleased smile, Isabelle rose and instructed her nephew, the bank's president, to contact Donovan as soon as possible. His was a giant undertaking and should be started immediately.

"And by the way," she said, picking up her alligator bag, "I'm sure he'll want to make some renovations to the house. See that he has the money for that, too." With a benign smile, she had turned and exited the boardroom, leaving behind the scent of Tabu and defeat.

Wes was the only one smiling as his great-aunt sailed out of the room with all the inherent arrogance of royalty. Wes had always known she was a piece of work, and her actions that morning proved it. She must have been hell on wheels as a young woman, he thought. He would have liked to have known her then.

At exactly ten minutes after the showdown, Wes was back in the office. Over a lunch of barbecue and fries, Wes laughingly told Reed what had happened. Reed laughed along with Wes, but inside he felt a niggling discomfort. It was only after his unconventional partner left for his own office that the significance of Donovan Delaney's moving back hit Reed.

As terrible as Hutch Delaney had been, Donovan had never done anything that might make Reed believe he was anything like his father. Actually, he and the younger Delaney had traveled down similar roads as young men. The only difference was that, despite his reputation for having quick fists and liking fast cars and faster girls, rumor had it that Donovan never so much as touched anything containing alcohol, something Reed couldn't claim. Reed had no problem with Donovan moving back. The problem was that if Donovan moved back, his sister would come to visit, and just the thought of running into Sophie again was enough to make his blood boil.

He was the first to admit he was partly at fault for what had happened. He'd asked her out for the same reason Wes had asked out her cousin: both girls had a reputation for being easy, and he and Wes were only too anxious to see if the rumors were true. Reed never knew if Wes scored with Justine or not, but after three dates, he'd worked his way past all Sophie's objections. It hadn't been the thrill he expected.

She'd been a virgin, and she'd cried, and he'd felt an overwhelming guilt because he'd taken her virginity and she'd said she loved him. When he'd taken her home, she'd even told him she'd never be sorry it happened.

Even though Reed's guilt and the fear of his father's wrath had kept him from contacting her for more than a week, he'd finally succumbed to temptation and phoned. But just as he'd asked if the number he'd reached was the Delaney residence, his father had come into the room, and he'd slammed down the receiver.

Reed had been smart enough to lie. Instead of saying he was calling Sophie, he'd said he was calling Hutch Delaney to see if he'd give him the name of his bootlegger so he could buy some beer for a party Wes was throwing. The county was dry, but there were a couple of people who made good livings shipping alcohol in from Hot Springs or Texarkana, marking it up to satisfy those in want—or need.

"If you wanted to know where to buy liquor, why didn't you ask me?" Rowland said, suspicion gleaming in his eyes.

With his heart racing, Reed attempted a smile and another lie. "It isn't the sort of thing a guy generally asks his dad."

"Well, ask anyone but Hutch Delaney. The man is poison, and I want you to stay clear of him and his whole family."

Other than to tell him he should take Lara Grayson to the upcoming festival, that had been the end of the conversation and the incident. Then, one night a few weeks later, Reed had come home from Wes's and found his father waiting for him. Looking him squarely in the eyes, Rowland told Reed that Donovan Delaney had been beaten badly by his father.

Ruby had brought him to the emergency room, where Rowland happened to be treating one of his own patients.

Reed felt his stomach knot. "Why?"

"His mother says he came home and found Hutch hitting his sister."

Reed flinched at the words and, picturing Hutch's hamlike hands slapping Sophie's pretty face, groped for a nearby chair.

"Why?" was all he could think to say again.

"Evidently Hutch Delaney considers working over various members of his family some kind of sport."

Rowland was a hard man, and to rile him was a frightening thing, but he'd never struck Reed. It was difficult, if not impossible, for him to imagine a father abusing his family with his fists.

"You haven't heard anything about why he'd hit his girl, have you?"

Rowland's question jerked Reed's thoughts back, and his gaze found his dad's. There was a searching expression in Rowland's dark eyes that made Reed uncomfortable. He had the inexplicable feeling that somehow Rowland had found out about the night with Sophie. He swallowed. Prevaricated. "Like what?"

Rowland shrugged, his expression waiting...detached. "Don't play games with me, boy. I know you took her out at least once."

Stunned, all Reed could say was "How—"

"I have my ways. What I want to know is why?"

Angry at his dad, angrier at himself, Reed snapped, "Why do you think? I heard she was easy."

Surprisingly, Rowland smiled. "And was she?"

Reed didn't want to talk to his dad about his time

with Sophie. Even mentioning her name in his presence seemed like some sort of desecration to the memory of their time together. Now his guilt manifested itself in anger. "Easy enough."

Satisfied by the answer, Rowland had smiled again, risen from his chair. "Delaney said that if his dad ever touched his sister again, he'd kill him," Rowland said, and left Reed with his thoughts.

Reed imagined he'd seen a hint of weariness in his dad's shoulders he'd never seen before. And he looked older, somehow. Probably a trick of the light. Rowland Hardisty would never get old, never got tired. He would outlive them all.

A week later Hutch Delaney was dead, and Donovan was taken into custody. Donovan had come home to see history repeating itself, and he'd stuck to his vow.

Reed had tried once to call Sophie the next day, but the phone had been answered by a woman, probably her mother. He hadn't wanted to explain why he wanted to talk to Sophie, so he'd pretended he had the wrong number.

The shooting was the main topic of conversation for the next few weeks. During that time he also learned that Sophie had left town to go live with an uncle in Louisiana. The thought of never seeing her again hurt more than Reed thought possible or expected.

The pain of her leaving had been replaced with a new emotion when she returned to town for the trial, squiring a new husband and sporting a protruding belly. Reed's pain had given way to fury. She must have slept with this guy—or someone—the minute she stepped off the bus at Shreveport.

He never gave a single thought to the possibility that the baby might be his, and if he had, he would have dismissed it—after all, they'd only done it once. Nor did he consider how the news of his marriage to Lara Grayson might have affected Sophie. All he could think of was that her vow of love was nothing but a lie.

Four days after her conversation with Cassidy, Sophie was sitting at the kitchen table sipping a cup of cooling tea and wondering if she'd suffered a moment of insanity by agreeing to go back to Lewiston, when the phone rang, splintering the silence and scattering the memories. She picked up the receiver, answering as she did at the office. "This is Dr. Carlisle."

"Dr. Carlisle, indeed," drawled a husky, feminine voice. "This is your long-lost redneck cousin."

"Justine?" Sophie said with a laugh of pure delight.

"None other."

The throaty, Lauren Bacall voice Justine had been blessed with, along with a talent for putting words and music together was the combination that had helped her reach her current pinnacle of success in Nashville. Two years ago, after years of singing backup for the big-name singers and selling the occasional song, Justine had cut a demo at the insistence of friends and been signed with a major recording company. Her first CD had gone platinum. She had become, as she laughingly told Sophie, an overnight success seventeen years in the making.

But despite Justine's unfailing, often biting humor and the growing size of her bank account, Sophie knew her cousin was unhappy. What she didn't know was what lay at the root of that unhappiness. Though they'd been close growing up, they'd grown apart when Justine left home, and she showed no sign of sharing her problems with her psychologist cousin.

"How are you?" Sophie asked now, the memory of their youthful closeness a sharp ache in her heart.

"I'm at the top of the charts, darlin'."

It didn't escape Sophie's notice that Justine's answer made a comment about her professional life instead of her personal one.

"How about you? Is everything okay?" Justine asked. "I've had this uncanny feeling I should call all afternoon."

"Must be your ESP," Sophie said. "I've been wallowing in thoughts of the past."

"Good grief. Have you broken out the Valium, yet?"

Sophie laughed. Justine could always make her laugh. "It wasn't that bad."

"Yes, it was," Justine replied. "And if you don't think so, you should go talk to a shrink about your delusions and denial."

Sophie laughed again. "You're right, of course. It was a nightmare."

"A living hell," Justine concurred. "So what prompted your little trip down memory lane?"

Sophie hesitated, wondering if she should tell Justine Donovan's plans, wondering what her cousin would say to his suggestion that she and Cassidy move back to Arkansas.

"Donovan has decided he wants to buy my part of Mama's place and put in a bunch of greenhouses."

"He wants to move back?" Justine cried, disbelief ringing in her voice.

"You know Donovan. He never was one to dance to the same tune as everyone else. He says that's home to him, and he feels like he paid his debt to society…" Sophie's voice faltered. No, Donovan had paid *her* debt to society. "So he should be able to live wherever he pleases."

"He'll still be Hutch Delaney's kid."

"I know, but he's made his decision, and you know as well as I do that once he's made up his mind, there's no changing it."

"I do recall that," Justine said in a dry tone. "So how do you feel about the news?"

"The same way you do," Sophie said. "I'll miss him terribly, and Cassidy is devastated. He's the closest thing she has to a father since Jake died." A brief silence stretched over the phone lines, and finally Sophie said, "He wants us to go back, too."

Instead of the explosion of disbelief she expected, Justine said, "I sort of suspected he would, since the two of you are so close."

"I told him it was impossible with my practice and Cass so settled in high school and everything. But we are going to go along to help him get moved in."

"A girl's gotta do what a girl's gotta do," Justine wisecracked. "And don't start prying about why I've never been back myself. Save your professional ear for someone who needs it."

It was an old argument. Sophie had her suspicions about why her cousin had left Lewiston but didn't say anything. "I have a feeling that someone who needs it is you," she said in a gentle voice. "And Aunt Opal misses you. You used to be so close. Whatever happened between the two of you, it would help if you talked about it."

"It might, and then again, maybe it wouldn't. I'm a survivor, just like you, Doc, and since you're worried about my relationship with Mama, let me ease your mind. I've managed to see her every few years since I left, and I send her money on a regular basis."

"Okay," Sophie said, hearing the anger in her cousin's voice. It was time to change the subject. "So, how was Chicago?"

Justine didn't speak for a moment. "Why did you ask about Chicago?" she said, finally. "That was four months ago."

"I don't know," Sophie said, puzzled by the irritation she heard in her cousin's voice. "I just haven't talked to you in ages, and it was the first thing that came to mind. Bad gig?"

"No," Justine corrected. "Actually, the ticket sales were phenomenal. Not a sellout, but close. I just did something stupid while I was there, that's all."

"Something stupid" was how Justine generally referred to succumbing to the lure of alcohol. Seeing how liquor had ruined Sophie's family's life, and after making a fool of herself the one time she'd gotten drunk as a teenager had made Justine, like Donovan and Sophie, swear off alcohol. Sometimes, though, on the extremely rare occasion, Justine had a drink or two. She was always penitent and always swore she'd done or said something outrageous and terrible, even though she usually hadn't.

"So you had a couple of drinks and danced on the tables, huh?" Sophie teased, knowing Justine probably wouldn't tell her any more about this incident than she would about why she wouldn't go back to Lewiston.

"It was worse than dancing on the table." Sophie

heard the resigned sigh that whispered through the phone lines. "But I'm definitely paying the fiddler."

There was a heaviness in her cousin's voice that broke Sophie's heart. Something was eating at her. Something big. "Why don't you come see me?"

"Not now, Sophie," Justine said, a note of weariness creeping into her voice. "Pete and I are having some disagreements about my basic philosophies of life."

What the heck was that supposed to mean? Sophie wondered. Pete Bennett was Justine's manager. Incredibly savvy about the business, aggressive and very controlling, Pete was the one responsible for Justine's meteoric rise to the top of the country charts. Sophie was inclined to think that if Justine's career was in good shape, her personal beliefs were none of Pete's business, unless, of course, they interfered with her work. And what might interfere in her work? A man. *Ah…* If she was interested in someone, Pete would no doubt believe that she should be concentrating on her singing, not squandering her time with a man.

"So you ticked him off about something," Sophie said, knowing better than to put her thoughts into words. "He'll get over it."

"I don't think so."

Sophie gritted her teeth against a rush of irritation. "Look," she said, out of patience with her cousin. "Why don't you stop with the innuendo. You either want to tell me what's going on, or you don't."

"Fine," Justine snapped. "If you must know, I'm pregnant."

"Pregnant?" Sophie echoed, stunned by the news. If she hadn't been sitting, she'd have sought a chair.

"Too big a word for you, Doc?" Justine asked in a sarcastic voice. "You know? With child. Knocked up."

Knocked up. The words played through Sophie's mind in Hutch's voice, bringing back the memory of the shame she heard in her cousin's. She connected a couple of mental dots. "*That's* what happened in Chicago."

"Oooh, smart lady. Yeah, that's what happened in Chicago. Two glasses of vermouth and what's left of my virtue goes down the tubes. And don't ask me who it was."

"I wouldn't dare," Sophie asked, reeling from the news. "I gather this is what's causing the strain between you and Pete."

"He wants me to have an abortion. I told him if Faith could work a career around having babies, so could I. He pointed out that Faith's career was a little more established than mine, and that she has a husband." Justine sighed. "He says I need to be touring, building sales, and I can't tour eight months' pregnant. He may be right, but I can't not have this baby, Sophie. It's a part of…me."

"I know." The two softly spoken words said it all.

"Yeah, you do, don't you?"

Other than Sophie's immediate family, the only ones who'd known about her pregnancy had been Justine, the first one she'd confided in, and Justine's mom. Not even her stepuncle had known what the altercation had been about, the night Hutch was killed. "You don't regret keeping her?" Justine asked.

"How could anyone have any regrets over giving birth to Cassidy?"

"Good enough for me. Besides, it's too late to do anything now, anyway. Pete can yell and scream all he wants. I hired him to deal with my problems. At best, life's a crapshoot. If it all goes down the tubes, I made a pretty good living writing songs and singing backup before I started singing."

"That's the spirit," Sophie said, glad to hear the defiance replace the depression in Justine's voice.

Justine laughed and changed the topic of conversation back on Sophie. "So, you're going back to Lewiston."

"For two weeks," Sophie said.

Justine laughed. "You can deny it all you want, Doc, but you're hoping you'll run into Reed Hardisty again."

Sophie had no smart comeback. As much as the thought of bumping into Reed threw her into a tizzy, she had a sneaking suspicion her cousin was right.

Chapter Three

The trip to Lewiston was a long one. Donovan, Sophie and Cassidy, along with a friend of Donovan's, had loaded the rental truck the day before and headed north at daybreak. Cassidy made part of the trip in the truck with her uncle and part with Sophie, who was driving Donovan's sports utility vehicle.

When they arrived, Sophie couldn't help noticing that the only things different from when she'd been there for Ruby's funeral in late October were the colors of the grass and the coating of dust that had settled over the scarred furniture during the winter and spring.

She opened up the windows to banish the stale scent that accompanied a house too-long vacant, then the three of them took a tour of the place, while Donovan explained his ideas for renovation. Sophie agreed that when he was finished, there would be little resemblance to the place that held so many bad memories.

Outside, he pointed out the spot where he planned to build his greenhouses and explained what he planned to do, but no matter how hard she tried, Sophie couldn't share his enthusiasm. It was hard to get past the fact that she was losing her brother.

Deciding that they were too tired to start unloading until the following day, too tired even to throw a sandwich together, Donovan and Cassidy opted to go into Lewiston and grab some burgers for dinner. Sophie stayed behind to find the paper plates and turn on the window air-conditioning units to start cooling down the house for the night.

As she waited for them to return, she sat in her mother's porch swing and gazed at the pastoral scene rolling out before her. Beyond a field of lush coastal Bermuda grass that needed to be cut and baled, a gravel drive meandered through a thick stand of pine and hardwood to the highway that led to Crescent Lake, so named because of its shape. In the spring, the greening woods would be splashed with spatters of snowy-white dogwood and draped with clusters of grapelike wisteria blossoms.

The memory brought the ache of homesickness to her heart. Not for any person or place, but for the sweet simplicity of summer days when the air was filled with the scent of fresh-cut hay, dust motes and the sass of a mockingbird's song. Days when the sounds of her mother and her aunt's conversation were punctuated by the clank of canning jars and the fruity aroma of peeled peaches or the sharp scent of the vinegar and pickling spices. Times when she and Justine had swung barefoot in the porch swing while sipping water through green onion tops—what Donovan dubbed a poor man's drinking straw. Evenings when june bugs prowled the window screens, and the muted sounds of the television provided a background for the bullfrogs and crickets as the day slipped into night, and the fireflies came out to dazzle the fairies.

Battling a sorrow she didn't understand, Sophie went to refill her water glass. As always, walking into the kitchen was like stepping through a door and going back in time. After Hutch's death, Ruby had been too busy keeping a roof over her head to bother much with decorating, and much of what was in the house had been there since long before Sophie escaped to a better life. A plastic dish drainer sat in the sink. The stove, a relic from the fifties, given to the Delaneys by Ruby's mother, was spotless. There was no dishwasher, no microwave. Ruby Delaney was more apt to eat a bowl of cereal or some cold corn bread and milk for a meal than a prepackaged microwave meal.

As she had often lately, as the mother of a sixteen-year-old, Sophie felt a longing—not for her old life but for an uncomplicated lifestyle and an innocence that had vanished as surely as the dodo. She was sorry she and Jake had never given Cassidy a sister to share life's pains and pleasures. Sorry Donovan had never given Cassidy a cousin to share her joys and woes the way Justine had Sophie's. Sorry they'd lived so far away and that Cass had never had the opportunity to really know what a special woman her grandmother had been.

The thought of Ruby brought a sharp pang of sorrow. Ruby Delaney had been a good woman, who deserved far better than what life had handed her. Ruby and her twin sister, Opal, had both managed to marry the wrong kind of man—in her aunt's case, twice. Hutch Delaney was an abuser of both alcohol and his family. Aunt Opal's first husband had been a womanizer; her second was a born gambler and con artist as well as a man who liked variety in his women.

Sophie had never understood why her mother had stayed with her dad, but after Cassidy was born, Ruby had confessed that even when things were their worst, she'd had faith that Hutch would stop drinking and return to being the man he'd once been—the good man who'd laughed and teased.

Years before, when the sisters had found themselves pregnant, their due dates only weeks apart, they had decided to give their children—should they be girls—names that would lift them above their humble backgrounds. Ruby Delaney had chosen Sophia, for her favorite actress, Sophia Loren. Opal had picked Justine, simply because she liked the sound of it.

Hutch, who'd been a model husband and sober back before the logging accident that had taken his leg when Sophie was eight, had laughed when Ruby told him what she wanted to name their second child, and inevitably everyone except Ruby had shortened Sophia to Sophie. Donovan had called her Sophe from the beginning.

Born just three weeks apart, the cousins had grown up with the closeness of sisters. It had seemed only natural that when Reed Hardisty had asked Sophie for a date, his friend, Wes Grayson, had asked out Justine. Reed had been twenty and in college at the University of Arkansas. Sophie was sixteen and, like her cousin, well developed. She and Justine should have known what Reed and Wes wanted from them, and maybe on some level they did, but the temptation to taste a bit of the good life had been too strong for either of them to turn down the invitation and the heartache that was bound to follow.

As an adult who'd undergone a lot of counseling for the events in her past, Sophie realized that what she'd once felt for Reed hadn't been mature love at all, but a natural desire to try to grab hold of the unattainable. What they'd shared had been curiosity and a teen's fixation about the very thing they'd been cautioned not to do. In Sophie's case, there was also a desire to feel wanted, if only for a while and even if that wanting was for all the wrong reasons. She knew now that her wants and needs were not unlike those of millions of other young people.

She'd also come to realize that if Reed had used her, she'd done the same with him, hoping against hope that he would see beyond her outer trappings, see her for the person she was inside, not just as Hutch Delaney's girl in the homemade clothes. During their brief courtship, she'd prayed with a fervency that had surprised her that Reed would grow to love her and take her away from the house where the slightest misstep might result in bruises and welts.

But it hadn't happened. Instead, Sophie had been robbed of another bit of naiveté and forced into adulthood long before she should have been. She'd thought the last trace of her innocence had vanished when she'd pulled the trigger that had taken her father's life, but it had been the phone call from Rowland Hardisty mere days after the incident, urging her to take the money he knew she had, to leave town and build herself a "new, better life" that had killed her gullibility for good. She'd hung up knowing once and for all that for girls like her there were no white knights, no easy ways out, no brass rings. There was nothing out there but more of what she'd grown up with. She'd left Lewiston with Hardisty money in her fake-leather purse and her heart protected by a hard armor of self-preservation. She wouldn't be so easily taken in the next time.

Then she'd met Jake.

She'd been in Bossier City, Louisiana, for less than a week when, after realizing she couldn't get a waitress position where they served liquor because of her age, she'd lied on her application and secured a job working at a popular seafood restaurant. For once she was glad she'd developed early and wasn't bubbly and giddy acting. Remembering her upbringing, she'd felt guilty about the lie, but rationalized it by telling herself she had to make a living for herself and her baby, and the tips would be much better at a nice restaurant.

Jake, who'd grown up in Springhill, was attending Louisiana State University in Shreveport with the aid of scholarships, loans and grants. He supplemented his income with the tips he made waiting tables.

Unlike Sophie, Jake knew exactly what he wanted and where he was going. Born to a loving mother who was a teacher and a father who was a mechanic and also a deacon at their church, Jake had the belief in himself that came with a stable homelife and a decent upbringing. Attractive, friendly and outgoing, he attacked every aspect of his life with the same enthusiasm and dedication—whether it was studying for finals or waiting tables.

A person who truly liked other people, he joked with the customers, never forgot a name, could spout off the specials with ease and had no trouble remembering who ordered what or any small adjustments or variations that might be made to the order. He was tipped well. Sophie, on the other hand, was too introverted to feel comfortable in her job. Though she was pleasant and agreeable, she had to write everything down and was tipped pretty much the expected minimum.

After the first few nights, Jake took her under his wing and gave her some advice on how to use associations to boost her memory. It helped, but nothing he said could help her overcome her timidity, so she never became nearly as good as he was. It was only after they were married that she learned he had an eidetic memory.

He'd asked her out that first week, but Sophie had declined. As cute and friendly as he was, and as much as she enjoyed being with him, she couldn't forget that she loved Reed Hardisty and was expecting his baby—not the sort of thing you told prospective suitors, no matter how easygoing they might be.

Jake was nothing if not persistent. When, after the second week he still refused to take no for an answer, Sophie had blurted out the truth in desperation: she was pregnant by a guy back in Arkansas. She wasn't interested in dating anyone. The confession deterred Jake for all of three days.

The next time he had approached her, it was with a new plan of attack: would she like to share an apartment?

"Are you crazy?" she'd responded.

"Look," he said. "It's perfect. You're living on a shoestring. So am I. You're pregnant by someone else, and you love the guy. I respect that. But it would be easier on both of us if we got a two bedroom apartment and shared expenses—and chores. I'll do my part of the cleaning and cooking." He sketched an X over his heart. "Promise. Besides, if we move in together, you'll have someone to take you to the hospital when the baby comes."

It had taken him more than a week, but Sophie had finally agreed. She still didn't know why. Jake Carlisle had been a stranger. All-American good looks aside, he might have been a rapist or a murderer. But when she was with him, things always seemed a bit brighter, and he always managed to coax a laugh from her. Since laughter had been in short supply at the Delaney house, it was a nice feeling.

They'd found a reasonably priced, two-bedroom, two-bath apartment and moved—against Sophie's better judgment and his parents' wishes—furnishing it with pieces picked up from Goodwill and the Salvation Army. The arrangement had worked out remarkably well. Sophie felt safe for the first time in a long time and very nearly happy, yet the closer it came to the time she had to go back to Lewiston for the trial, the more depressed she became.

There was no way she could disappear for days and not tell Jake the reason, so, finally, she'd offered him the same version of what had happened the night of Hutch's death that she and Donovan had told the authorities.

Not only had Jake been dumbfounded, he'd pulled her into his arms and cried. For the first time in her life, Sophie felt that someone outside her immediate family cared about what happened to her. When she touched the tears on his cheeks in wonder, she'd felt something inside her shift toward a fuller understanding of mature love, and she'd begun to love Jake a little for caring. When she'd told him she had to go back for the trial, he'd understood that she was upset because she would have to face the town pregnant and unmarried.

"And you might see him—this Reed Hardisty."

She nodded.

"I guess you'd rather not have him think you're pining away for him, even if it is the truth," Jake stated, taking her hands.

Sophie tightened her fingers around his, thankful for his friendship and support. "I'd rather die than let him know he's caused me one second's pain," she said, a rare hardness in her eyes.

"Then show him he hasn't."

"How?"

"Take a husband when you go back to Lewiston." When she started to object, he held up a hand. "Think about it. He and his dad probably think you got rid of the baby. When they see you didn't, they'll have a moment's fear until they see how well dressed you are, and then meet your new husband. So this is about you being able to thumb your nose at them and their selfishness."

"You want to go with me? Pretend to be my husband?"

Jake shook his head. "I don't want to pretend. I want to marry you. I want to really be your husband and this baby's father."

Embarrassed, touched, ashamed, feeling like one of the stray animals he was so fond of rescuing, she blurted, "I don't want your pity!"

"You don't have it," he countered. "You have my admiration for being able to stay as decent as you have under the circumstances you've had to deal with. And you have my love.''

"Love?" she gasped, shocked by the very thought.

"Why not? Because it's too soon? We've lived together for almost three months. I know most of your bad habits by now, and you know mine." He'd lifted her hand to his lips and brushed a kiss across her knuckles. "Marry me, Sophie, and let me fight your battles for you."

It was tempting. Very tempting. But then, Sophie thought of him putting himself through school, of the way he worked late hours and studied later, surviving on fast food and a few hours' stolen sleep. "You have enough battles of your own."

He'd smiled at her. "My shoulders are broad enough to take on one more. Two," he'd corrected, with another grin. "It doesn't have to be a real marriage—not until you're ready for it to be. Not until you're over Reed. Marry me, Sophie. Please."

He'd told her later that he never begged. He'd also said he would have crawled over hot coals if it would have swayed her. In the end, she'd said yes, and she'd never regretted it.

They'd spent more money than they should have on clothes for their brief stay in Lewiston, but when they'd run into Reed's father, the stunned expression on his face made the extravagance worth it. Even though she was quaking inside, Sophie had taken a great deal of satisfaction in introducing Jake.

They hadn't come face-to-face with him again, but she had spotted Rowland Hardisty sitting in the back of the courtroom on two different occasions. On the day Donovan was sentenced, Sophie had left the courtroom crying and leaning on her new husband's arm. She'd seen Rowland approaching and thought he might be about to confront her, but something in her face must have stopped him, because he passed by without a word.

Sophie had been glad to put the trial behind her, and she and Jake settled into their married life. Probably because their marriage put an end to the stigma of their "living together," his parents accepted her as if their courtship and marriage had progressed through the usual phases. There were times, though, during those first few months when Sophie caught a worried expression on Sarah Carlisle's face. But when Cassidy was born, both of the elder Carlisles seemed as proud as if Jake had been the one to father her.

True to his word, Jake hadn't pressed for intimacy, waiting for Sophie to make the move, which she did when Cassidy was eight months old. By that time she'd figured out that there was a big difference between infatuation and love, physical desire and the desire to touch and be touched as a way of expressing deeper, mutual emotions.

For fourteen years her life had been as close to perfect as life on earth can be. For the most part her brief idyll with Reed Hardisty was remembered as a youthful mistake, something she'd done that she wasn't particularly proud of and for which she'd paid the price. It had taken years for the anger she felt toward him and his father to fade. Then there were those times—increasingly frequent since Jake died—that Sophie looked at Cassidy and saw something of Reed in her that sometimes prompted unwanted memories and a sudden, irrational quickening of her heart.

Was it the unexplained poignancy that accompanies recollections of the past, the way the mind has of wearing off the edges of the bad memories and replaying the good ones over and over? Was she still longing for something she could never have, or were the recollections prompted by frustrated sexual needs that hadn't been met since Jake's death?

After almost two years, Sophie didn't know, and she didn't want to examine the feelings too closely. Not tonight. She was on Reed's turf now.

The sound of the Explorer's engine preceded the vehicle that exploded around a bend in the road and ended the disquieting turn of Sophie's thoughts. Donovan was driving much too fast. The truck pulled to a stop in front of the house, and Cassidy—all long, bare legs and dark hair—emerged with a smile.

"You were driving way too fast down that gravel road," Sophie said to her brother.

"Sorry."

He didn't look sorry. He looked angry, or at the very least irritated. Sophie wanted to ask him what had happened during their short trip to town—had he accidentally bumped into Lara?—but didn't want to broach the subject with Cassidy around.

"He had to drive fast, Mom," Cassidy said, seemingly unaware of the tension that oozed from her uncle. "We didn't want the stuff to get cold. We got *tons* of food. Burgers and fries with chili and cheese and onion rings and milk shakes—which is another reason Uncle Donovan was driving so fast. We didn't want them to melt."

Sophie forced a smile. "One excuse is as good as another, I suppose." She reached for a bag and headed for the door. "Let's divvy this stuff up. I'm starving."

With paper plates piled high on TV trays, they sat

on the porch and watched the sun slide slowly into day's end. It seemed that with the lessening of light, the tautness left Donovan's body, and the tightness in his jaw eased. It wasn't long before he was smiling and, along with Cassidy and Sophie, was making the occasional comment about how good the fast food tasted.

"We must be starving or crazy to think this stuff tastes good," Sophie said, propping her feet up on the porch railing and picking up a forkful of chili-cheese fries.

"We are," Donovan said with a smile.

"What?"

"Starving *and* crazy," he said.

Cassidy drew a deep breath. "Maybe it's the country air. It smells good here."

"Smells like rain," Donovan said.

"You can't smell the rain," she said.

"Sure I can. It smells like wet earth or something." He shrugged. "It's something sort of…fecund in the air, something that promises that things will flourish."

Sophie looked at him in a bit of surprise. Donovan wasn't one for flowery phrases. "The country brings out the poet in you, brother, dear."

Donovan looked embarrassed, an emotion seldom seen on his rugged features. "I just hope it brings out the grower in me."

"It will."

Cassidy slurped the last dregs of her milk shake and stood. "I can't eat another bite, and I'm exhausted. I'm going to take a shower and turn in."

"So early?"

"Gimme a break, Mom. We got up before daylight."

"Yeah, we did, and I won't be far behind you. I was just giving you a hard time. Will you take my plate, too?"

"Sure. Are you finished, Uncle Donovan?"

"You can take my plate, but I'm gonna eat the rest of your mom's fries."

Sophie regarded her brother in surprise. He'd already had two burgers, an order of chili-cheese fries, onion rings and a side salad. Of course, he was the original junk food junkie as well as a bottomless pit. "How can you eat so much?" she asked.

"I'm a growing boy."

"Well, you certainly have a magnificent metabolism," Sophie said as she helped her daughter gather the remaining food.

"I work it off. You burn a lot of calories working outside in the heat."

"I guess you would. Thanks, honey," she said to Cassidy, who swung the door open and stepped inside. "See you in the morning." The door closed behind Cassidy, and Sophie smiled at her brother. "Well, we've been here over two hours and she isn't bored yet."

"Give her a little credit. She's more together than a lot of girls her age."

"She wants a tattoo."

Donovan almost choked on a bite of fries. "A tattoo?"

"Yeah. Just a small one where no one will see it when she's dressed."

"Then what's the point?"

"That's what I said."

"Don't worry," Donovan said. "I can nip that one in the bud."

"Be my guest."

Donovan finished off the fries and set the container and plastic fork aside. As Cassidy had, he slurped up the remainder of his milk shake. Then, without preamble, he said, "We saw Reed at the Dairy Delight."

The announcement robbed Sophie of breath. "Cassidy?"

"Was very polite."

"Polite?"

"We literally ran into him. I didn't have much choice but to make introductions."

"Did he—"

Donovan shook his head. "Trust me, though he may be smart, the man doesn't have a clue Cass is his daughter."

"Thank God."

"Yeah." Donovan stared unseeingly at a place in the distance before saying, "He had his little girl with him."

Sophie didn't know why the idea of Reed having another daughter should cause her a second's pain, but it did. "I knew he and Lara had a daughter," she said, "but I don't think I've seen her."

"She's a cute kid," Donovan said. "Probably eleven or twelve. She has a smile like Lara's."

There was no pain in Donovan's voice; there was an undeniable wistfulness. Sophie felt another of those nagging pangs of guilt. If Donovan hadn't taken the blame for what she'd done, maybe he and Lara could have had a future.

"Do you want to tell me what happened with you two?" Sophie prompted. She knew her brother. If she kept at him, he would talk—when he was good and ready.

Donovan sighed and gave a negligent shrug. "Not much to tell. We were an item, but no one knew about it. My idea, not hers. When I was arrested and went to jail I broke it off. She married Reed in a matter of weeks. End of story."

"But not the end of what you felt for her."

Donovan rubbed his chin in contemplation. "I guess I misjudged what we felt for each other. If she'd really cared for me, she wouldn't have married Reed so soon."

"It's called rebound, Donovan. And it may have been something else entirely."

He lifted one heavy eyebrow. "Yeah? Like what?"

"Like maybe Rowland Hardisty and Phil Grayson forced them into it."

"Sophe, honey," Donovan said with exaggerated patience. "This isn't the nineteenth century. Fathers don't arrange marriages anymore."

Sophie shrugged. "All I know is that Reed told me it was both Rowland's and Phil's dearest wish that he and Lara get together. They even dated for a while, but Reed told me they just weren't right for each other."

"People change."

"They do," she agreed. "But not so much in such a short period of time."

"So why would the two old guys push them into marriage, and why would Reed and Lara let them?"

It was Sophie's turn to shrug. "I've given this a lot of thought over the years, and if I had to hazard a guess, I'd say Rowland would have been wanting to do something to make Reed forget all about me and our baby. A new wife and a move out of town would go a long way toward that goal. Who knows?

Reed might have been as gung ho for the idea as his dad. If he married someone else, someone suitable, he'd figure I'd lose interest in staking some sort of claim on him myself.''

''But why would Lara's dad go along with it?''

''Who knows? Rowland and Phil were good friends. To join the two families, maybe?'' A sudden thought occurred to her. ''If Lara was upset about you not seeing her, she might not have cared what happened and let her dad push her into it,'' Sophie offered.

Donovan's mouth quirked in a crooked grin. ''I guess it really doesn't matter after all this time.'' He stretched mightily and stood. ''I'm beat. Do you want to shower first?''

Sophie shook her head. ''Go ahead. I think I'll sit out here for a while.'' She smiled. ''I was thinking about Mama earlier. The way things used to be. It wasn't a bad life until Dad lost his leg.''

''Even then Mom never lost her faith that things would change. She was a real saint.'' Sophie couldn't answer for struggling with her tears. Donovan cleared his throat. The emotions hovering in the darkness were thick enough to cut with a knife. ''I'm going in.''

''See you in the morning,'' she said huskily. ''Good night.''

Donovan brushed her cheek with a kiss and turned to go inside. The door was about to close behind him when she called, ''Don't use all the hot water.''

''I won't.''

Alone, with no sounds but the rustle of the wind through the pine trees, the symphony of frogs and crickets and the occasional yelp of a coyote, Sophie found her thoughts going to Reed once more. Suddenly the sparkle of headlights glittered through an opening in the trees. Who on earth would be coming to visit at this time of night?

She didn't have long to wait to find out. She had no idea what kind of car it was that came purring down the lane, only that it was low-slung and clearly expensive. It pulled to a stop in front of the house, and the driver opened the door.

Sophie got a brief glimpse of a male profile in the flash of the car's interior light before the man got out. Her heart seemed to stop beating, and she found herself struggling for her next breath of air. Even though it had been seventeen years since she'd seen him, there was no doubt as to the identity of her late-night visitor. The man walking toward her was none other than Reed Hardisty.

Chapter Four

Reed stopped at the bottom of the short flight of steps leading to the porch and thrust his hands into the pockets of his pricey gray slacks. Stunned to immobility, Sophie gripped the arms of the rocker and stared at him. She wasn't aware that her heart had begun to beat faster, only that her mouth felt as dry as two-day-old toast. She scoured her mind for some sin she might have committed that would cause God to send Reed as her punishment.

It filled her with dismay to see that his body hadn't gone soft and fat the way she'd wished for him to do on nights she'd lain awake meting out various retributions for the way he'd used and abandoned her. Instead, his body looked fit and firm beneath the slacks and the short-sleeved dress shirt. His face had fared well, too. The faint light from the kitchen window cast his features into sharp planes and angles that revealed the classic sculpting of his bones, a few creases on his forehead and a fanning of lines at the corners of his eyes.

"Hello, Sophie."

His voice hadn't changed much. Its tonal qualities were, perhaps, deeper, but it was still rich and soft and, heaven help her, it still sent a shiver of awareness quivering down her spine.

The idea that he could evoke any response from her other than anger, brought that emotion to the forefront. "What are you doing here?" she demanded.

"I came to see Donovan."

Donovan? Though they were of an age, Donovan had never been bosom buddies with Reed Hardisty. "He's gone to bed. What could you possibly want with my brother, anyway?"

Reed seemed taken aback by her icy demeanor, but the manners he'd been taught at his socialite mother's knee stood him in good stead. "I'd heard through the grapevine that he was moving back to Lewiston, doing some remodeling and putting in some greenhouses. After I ran into him and your daughter at the Dairy Delight, I started thinking about a friend's new construction company. They need the work, and I know firsthand that they're reputable. I thought I'd pass the word."

It never even crossed her mind that Reed could have called Donovan with the information. The only thing that registered was that he'd said *her* daughter. The fact that she'd been pregnant with his child when she left town seemed to have slipped his mind. The idea that she and Cassidy had been forgotten so easily upped her ire a notch. She leaped to her feet. "Since when do you give a tinker's damn about Donovan? About any Delaney?''

''When did you become such a shrew?'' he countered in a voice that said he'd already had enough of her waspishness.

Sophie gasped in surprise and clutched at the porch railing to steady herself. Not only had she never heard a harsh word come from Reed's beautifully shaped lips, she was stunned by his assessment of her. Had she become a shrew? She didn't think so, but facing the one person who possessed the power to destroy the life she'd constructed with such care frightened her more than she would ever let him know. Anger was her only weapon to combat the fear.

''I'm sorry,'' he said, genuine contrition in his voice. ''That was uncalled for.''

''Yes, it was.'' Despite her resolve not to fall to pieces in front of him, Sophie felt tears burning beneath her eyelids.

''So was your comment.'' He mounted the steps, moving to within half a dozen steps of her.

A sense of preservation caused her to take a step back. Reed stopped short. He raked a hand through his hair in a well-remembered gesture. ''I should have called instead of driving out here.''

''Why didn't you?''

He shrugged. ''It was a spur-of-the-moment thing.''

''Have you grown spontaneous through the years, then? I thought everything in Reed Hardisty's life was planned, labeled and compartmentalized, and anything that might throw a kink in the status quo was gotten rid of, no matter what the cost.''

He understood at once what she was alluding to.

He exhaled, a harsh sound of frustration. "That was a long time ago, Sophie."

She sucked in a sharp breath, stunned by his blasé attitude, destroyed by his ability to have put the past so completely behind him while she was forced to face it every day. "How dare you." Her voice quavered with the intensity of her rage.

"How dare I what?" Reed snapped. "Bring up the past? I didn't. You did. That is what that little speech was all about wasn't it? Well, let me give you the same advice my daughter gives me. Get over it."

Clenching her jaw to keep from saying something she knew she'd regret, Sophie whirled and headed for the door. She wouldn't give him the satisfaction of knowing how much he'd hurt her—then or now.

She had her hand on the doorknob when he grabbed her upper arm and hauled her around to face him. She gave a little cry that had nothing to do with pain and everything to do with the sudden assault of memories. He'd done the very same thing the first time he'd kissed her. She looked up at him, wondering if he remembered, too.

The expression in his eyes was all the answer she needed. For the span of a few heartbeats, it might have been the summer of '83. His hands slipped up to her shoulders. He was so close she could feel the heat of his body. Or was that the heat that was rising from deep inside her, creeping throughout her like a prairie fire, hungrily licking up her brittle defenses and sober determination? As foolish as she knew it was, she stood silently, waiting to see what he might do next. Waiting…as she had so long ago, for some sign of acceptance.

Acceptance? She was an educated woman of independent means, respected in her field, with a high success rate of helping the people who came to her for guidance. She didn't need acceptance from anyone, least of all Reed Hardisty. When she realized how easily she had slipped back into the role of victim, she tried to pull free. "Let go of me."

Instead of complying, Reed met her angry gaze head-on. There was a puzzled look in his eyes, almost, she thought, as if he didn't understand her behavior. "We were kids, Sophie."

"That doesn't make it less real," she said, hating the breathless quality she heard in her voice.

"Oh, it was real, all right," he said.

His voice ended her struggles. It was soft and low pitched and filled with wonder and no small amount of pain, as if he'd just that instant realized the magnitude of what had happened between them and was struggling to understand it. The hard shell around her heart melted the slightest bit. She fought back the sudden urge to reach up and rub at the twin slashes of the frown that drew his dark eyebrows together, to whisper some word of comfort to him.

Then, as if he wanted to rid himself of the idea that there might have been more to what they shared than he was willing to acknowledge, Reed gave a decisive shake of his head. "We satisfied our mutual sexual needs."

The tender emotions she'd felt unfurling seconds before withered beneath a fury that rose inside her. It might not have been an adult love, and though it hadn't come close to what she'd felt for Jake, it had been just as real and as deep and pure as a young and tender sixteen-year-old heart could love. She thought about reminding him of Cassidy, but the very fact that he'd forgotten so easily stopped her.

Before she could think of a pithy reply, he released his hold on her and stepped back. The sudden removal of his hands brought a chill and a feeling of loss she couldn't have explained if she'd tried.

"Blake Meriweather," he said.

"What?" Lost in her thoughts, Sophie had no idea what he was talking about. What had she missed? She looked up at him, searching his face, but there was nothing readable in his eyes.

"Blake Meriweather is the man who owns the construction company. He's in the phone book. Tell Donovan I think he'll do a good job at a fair price." Without another word Reed turned and went down the steps, leaving Sophie to watch, her mouth hanging open in surprise.

She struggled to find something to say, but what? *Don't go?* Never! *Why are you leaving?* Worse. *Goodbye?* Stupid, under the circumstances. No, there was nothing to say after what had just happened between them, nothing to do but watch him get in his expensive car and drive away, his taillights growing dimmer and dimmer and finally disappearing beyond the thickness of the woods that stretched to the highway. Nothing to do but watch and bemoan the lapse in her defenses.

Shame and anger overwhelmed her. *He paid to be rid of you and Cassidy, and don't you forget it.* How could she have forgotten that fact for even a moment? How could she have felt one instant's tenderness for him?

And worse—how, after she'd known the love of a truly good man and experienced the joys of a wonderful marriage, could the nearness of someone so shallow and self-centered as Reed Hardisty have any effect on her? No man had stirred even a marginal awareness in her since she'd lost Jake and, until now, she'd begun to believe none would. For that man to be Reed was the cruelest of cosmic jokes.

Donovan would be quick to cut to the chase and say her reaction was normal, hormonal, her healthy body's need for attention after a lengthy abstinence. Maybe he would be right, but it didn't make the situation any more bearable, especially since she knew Reed for what he was—a user. He'd said himself that he'd used her to satisfy his sexual needs. When her pregnancy had complicated that, he'd run to his daddy for help, and Rowland had done what the rich are so good at doing: he'd bought Reed's way out.

The doorknob rattled, and Donovan stepped out onto the porch, wearing nothing but a pair of clean jeans. Thankful that his appearance put an end to her self-castigation and thoughts of Reed, Sophie's breathing came easier.

She regarded her brother with a faint smile of fondness. His wet hair was combed straight back from his face in a way that revealed the uncompromising masculinity of his facial structure. Tanned skin stretched over hard-earned muscles. Wide shoulders and taut thighs were covered by unfashionably snug denim. His perfect-macho image was ruined somewhat by the fact that he seemed surrounded by some sort of fruity aura.

She sniffed the air.

"Don't say a word," he commanded with a scowl and a pointing finger. "I couldn't find the bag with my shaving gear, and I had to use Cass's shampoo and stuff."

Sophie struggled to hold back a smile. "You smell, uh...good enough to eat. Strawberry?"

"With kiwi," he added, his own grudging smile tugging at one corner of his mouth. He plopped down in an ancient rocking chair a few feet away. "Why do women want to smell like fruit?"

"Beats me," Sophie told him. "I like flowers myself."

He grinned and reached over to lift the lid of the ice chest, rummaging around for his favorite soft drink. "There's nothing in here but juice."

"It's better for you than all those colas you drink."

"Yeah, but it'll be terrible with my Snickers bar."

Sophie smiled and shook her head. Donovan had a notorious sweet tooth. "Life's tough," she said with a shrug.

"And I thought you were one of those compassionate counselor types," he said, pulling a drink from the cooler. As he unscrewed the cap, he said, "I thought I heard you talking to someone."

Her brief, lighthearted mood vanished like the blinking of a distant firefly. "You did. It was Reed," she said before he could ask.

"Reed?" Disbelief underscored the question.

"Uh-huh," Sophie said. "He told me he knew you were moving back and renovating the house. It seems he knows someone who would give you a fair bid and do a good job."

"And who would that be?"

"Blake Meriweather."

"Blake Meriweather! He's in construction now?"

"Evidently he's just started his own company."

"You remember him, don't you? Sort of sandy hair. Looks like a linebacker. *Was* a linebacker in college."

"Lots of freckles?" she asked. "Always smiling?"

Donovan grinned. "That's Blake. I'll give him a call first thing in the morning."

He lifted his bare feet to the ice chest, stretched out his long legs and crossed his ankles. "So good old Reed drove all the way out here to tell someone he wouldn't normally give the time of day to about someone who might help him get established in the community." He took a long pull from the bottle of juice and shook his head. "I'm not buying it, Sophe."

"What do you mean?"

"I mean he didn't come out here to see me. He came to see you."

Though she'd been surprised by Reed's visit and questioned his reason, she'd never entertained the thought that he'd come to see her. It was a preposterous idea. One that made her heart rate accelerate the slightest bit, even as it filled her with dismay. "Me?"

"Yep."

"Why?"

Donovan shrugged. "Curiosity. He saw me and Cass at the Dairy Delight, saw how grown-up she is and started wondering how you'd fared through the years."

"He wanted to scope me out?" Sophie asked in shock.

"It's a normal reaction, Sis." One corner of Donovan's mouth lifted in a half smile. "I've never been prouder that you look so darn good."

"Thank you," Sophie said, pleased that her struggle to stay fit had paid off. "He didn't look too bad himself," she said before she thought about it.

Donovan took a swig of his juice. "Hmm. Is that interest I hear in your voice?"

"It is not."

"Come on, now. Don't tell me you haven't wondered a million times how Reed was weathering the years."

"Of course I have—not that I'm proud to have thought about him at all," she added primly. "But I'd never drive to his home on some sort of flimsy excuse, just to get a look at him."

"Of course you wouldn't."

While she understood Donovan's rationale, she didn't want to believe that Reed had deliberately sought her out. She'd prefer it if he kept his distance. It was all too much to think about. Weary from the drive and distressed by Donovan's theory, Sophie pushed herself to her feet. "I'm going to shower and go to bed."

"I won't be far behind you," Donovan said, popping the last of his candy bar into his mouth.

Sophie went inside. She wondered again if she'd made a mistake by allowing Donovan to talk her into coming back with him, even for a short time, and if he was right about the reason Reed had come out. She told herself she didn't give a darn one way or the other, but was honest enough to know she was lying to herself.

The next morning Sophie awoke just before dawn. She glanced at the clock and saw she'd been asleep less than three hours. Guilt was not conducive to rest, she thought, throwing her legs over the side of the bed and reaching for the short robe that matched her even shorter flower-sprigged gown. Even considering that it was purely hormonal, as Donovan suggested, her response to Reed's nearness had blindsided her. It wasn't like her to step into deep water when she knew the dangers lurking there. Not anymore.

Frustrated by her inability to understand her reaction to him, ashamed for what she considered her unfaithfulness to Jake and what they'd shared, she took a cup of coffee and left the stifling confines of the house. She wandered around the yard without purpose, noting the weed-filled flowerbeds with little interest, unmindful of the cheerful sounds of the summer because of the agonized refrain that pounded through her head—*Reed...Reed...Reed.*

What would Jake have thought about this turn of events? He wouldn't condemn her, that much was certain. Knowing him as she had, he would probably agree with Donovan and tell her that what she was feeling was normal. She and Reed had a past that bound them through a child they'd created together. Jake would smile that sweet smile of his and shrug.

"Don't fight it, babe," he would say. "You owe it to yourself to play out the hand you're dealt and see what happens." Jake was a big one for believing that things happened for a reason, no matter how much they threw one off track.

Somewhat calmed by the knowledge that he wouldn't condemn her for her momentary lapse, and with her psyche shored up against any further slip in the armor she'd donned to fortify herself against Reed, Sophie went back inside to see what she could stir up for breakfast, an almost impossible task with no milk or bread in the house.

She was looking for a date on some instant oatmeal when Cassidy strolled into the kitchen, rubbing her eyes, her long brown hair a tangle around her face. She was a beautiful girl, Sophie thought, somewhat dismayed by the womanly curves hiding beneath the boxer shorts and ragged T-shirt, which were Cassidy's sleeping apparel of choice. The realization that her daughter would be leaving for college in two more years brought a lump to Sophie's throat. She blinked fast and swallowed hard. "Good morning."

"'Morning."

"How did you sleep?"

"Like a log," Cassidy replied. "What's for breakfast?"

Though she wasn't particular about what it was—she'd eat leftover pizza or spaghetti as easily as cereal or a full breakfast—Cassidy was ready for food the minute her feet hit the floor.

"I was just looking around, trying to figure out what sort of resembles breakfast food."

"Nothing, huh?"

"There's some canned stuff, some flour with weevils, lumpy sugar, stale corn flakes, and some frozen Mexican dinners that probably need to be thrown out." She held up the small packet in her hand. "There's oatmeal."

Cassidy gave a shiver of distaste. "Ugh. I'll just have a cup of coffee for now. Where is Uncle Donovan?"

"I don't know," Sophie said, reaching for a cup. "The pickup is here, so I'd guess he's outside staking out the places he plans to put the greenhouses."

"Probably. Maybe he'll drive in and pick up something for breakfast."

"Better yet, why don't you throw on some clothes and drive in yourself," Sophie suggested. "You have your license, and if you can drive in Baton Rouge, you can certainly drive in Lewiston."

"Oh, wow! I never thought of that," Cassidy said.

"After breakfast you and I will drive to town and buy some groceries. I certainly don't intend to eat fast food for two weeks."

"Even *I* would get tired of fast food for two weeks," Cassidy said. "Especially since there's nothing but a burger chain and the Dairy Delight."

"Don't forget Martha's," Sophie said.

"Yeah, but Martha's isn't fast food," Cassidy reminded. "That's where you go when you want to have a sit-down dinner, a real luxury meal."

Sophie's lips quirked in a wry smile. "If you consider chicken and dressing, pork chops, beef tips and choice of three vegetables a luxury meal."

"It's my idea of heaven," Cassidy said. "Real meals are rare at our place."

The simple statement brought another of those twinges of guilt. There was a time they'd all worked together to fix dinner in a nightly ritual. After they'd lost Jake, she'd steered clear of the kitchen and taken on a heavier patient load. She'd found that the memories weren't so bad at the office. But working the long hours made fixing much more than a salad and casserole an impossibility. Cassidy had never complained, either about the food arrangement or the time Sophie spent at the office, so Sophie had assumed the new regime was okay with her daughter. Now she saw that in seeking to bury her own grief, she'd robbed Cassidy of time they could never get back.

"I've sort of slacked off in the mom department

since your dad died, haven't I?'' Sophie said, knowing she needed to hear Cassidy's response, knowing
Cassidy needed to say how she felt.

The look in her daughter's eyes was troubled and
a bit pleading, maybe even a little apologetic. ''I
don't really mind the meals, but like I said the other
day, it would be nice to spend more time together.''

With a cry of remorse, Sophie rounded the table
and put her arms around her daughter, hugging her
tightly. Cassidy held on as if she might never let her
go, a silent signal that she'd missed Sophie. After a
moment she stepped back and cradled Cassidy's face
in her palms. ''Oh, baby! I'm so sorry I haven't been
there for you the way I should have.''

''It's okay,'' Cassidy said, her own eyes growing
shiny.

''It's not okay.'' She smoothed Cassidy's tangled
hair back from her face. ''I didn't mean to shut you
out, and I'm going to see to it that things change as
soon as we get back home. I still miss your dad—I'll
always miss him, but it's time to join the living
again.''

If nothing else, Donovan's move had shown her
that, yet even as she made the promise, Sophie felt a
pang of disloyalty to Jake. But deep inside her, she
knew that the feeling was prompted more from her
uncertainty as to whether her decision was made out
of concern for her relationship with her daughter or
the fact that the mere sight of Reed made her feel
more alive than she had since her husband's death.

''You're going to get a life again, huh?'' Cassidy
said with a slight smile.

''It's time, don't you think?''

"I do. So you'll start going to the art galleries and the symphony again?"

"Yes."

"Will you…" Cassidy's voice trailed away.

"Will I what?" Sophie prompted.

"Start dating again?"

An image of Reed popped into her mind. She squelched it. "Would it bother you if I did?"

"I don't think so," Cassidy said with a shake of her head. "I've thought about it. You're still pretty, and I know you aren't old, so I guess it would be okay if it's the right guy—not some jerk."

"And who gets to decide if he's the right guy or a jerk?" Sophie asked with a lift of her eyebrows.

Cassidy shrugged. "I guess we'd have to decide together."

"Really?"

Cassidy grinned. "Okay, okay, you get to decide—" she held up a finger "—but I get to put my two cents worth in."

"Fair enough."

Cassidy gave Sophie another hug and said, "I'm going to get dressed and go get us some breakfast."

"Finally."

Reed sat hunched over an unread brief in his office, drinking a cup of cooling coffee and knowing that he'd lied to himself the night before. He'd told himself he would drive out to the Delaney place to give Blake Meriweather's name to Donovan and to show his support—a ridiculous idea since they'd never been friends—but all it had taken was one glimpse of Sophie sitting on the dark porch, the light from the kitchen window gilding her strawberry-blond hair, the fire of disdain lighting her eyes for him to realize that he'd gone for no other reason than to see her.

Though he'd known Donovan was coming back to town, it had come as a surprise to Reed when he and Belle had bumped into Delaney and his niece at the Dairy Delight. Donovan had aged, as Reed himself had, but considering that he'd had such a hard life and served time in prison, he'd fared well. Surprisingly he didn't seem bitter or hardened by his experiences. Instead, the satisfied expression in his eyes and his easy smile conveyed the picture of a man who was at complete ease with himself and his situation. Something Reed often wished for himself. Something he couldn't help but envy.

But it hadn't been seeing Donovan again that had shaken Reed as much as it had been seeing the girl. It had taken him just seconds to realize the stunning teenager was Sophie's daughter. Other than having brown hair, the girl—Cassidy—looked like Sophie at that age. Inexplicably, that realization had filled Reed with a driving desire to see Sophie again. He wanted to see if that hint of vulnerability still lurked in the depths of her blue eyes and if she'd let herself go the way so many of the women he'd gone to school with had. To see if the sight of her could still resurrect the feeling of invincibility she'd generated in him, a feeling he hadn't felt in a long time…maybe not since he'd dropped her off at the end of her lane seventeen years ago.

Not surprisingly, the only thing seeing her had resurrected was a sudden and powerful desire. She'd looked good. Too good. She was still pretty…prettier than she had been at sixteen. Her face, with its slightly square jawline, was more perfectly sculpted than when she was a girl, toned and refined by life. Her petite body was still slender, still curvy in all the right places. In a moment of pure déjà vu, he'd recalled the feel of that body in his arms, molded close, the satiny texture of bare flesh against flesh. The taste of it.

For an instant, the longing to feel that body wrapped around him one more time had become a painful ache. The unexpected desire had hit him like a hard jab to the gut, and he'd learned that, in spite of how she might feel about him, in spite of the fact that she'd lied about loving him, she still held the power to move him sexually.

It had been easy to make Sophie the villain for leaving town and marrying someone so soon after they'd stopped seeing each other, far easier to paint himself as the victim than to face the fact that he'd been the one to break off with her and know in his heart that he'd made a mistake.

He couldn't blame her for leaving town after the incident with her brother and father, but when she'd come back for the trial, married and pregnant, something inside Reed had twisted, turning what they'd shared into something hateful, hurtful. Despite his own role in how their relationship had played out, he'd felt the sting of betrayal.

When he'd expressed his fury to Wes the day Sophie and her husband had come back for the trial, Wes had accused him of being a dog in the manger.

"Sounds like you're jealous to me," Wes had said.

"I'm not jealous, but from the looks of her belly, it didn't take her too long to find herself someone to pick up where I left off."

"So you did sleep with her?" Wes's face had worn a sly grin.

"As if you didn't know."

"Hey," Wes said with a shrug, "I may have wondered, but you never said."

Wes had slapped him on the back and added philosophically, "You're the one who broke it off, buddy. You don't have any right to be ticked off because she moved on…unless you're still interested. And even if you are, I'd say you're about seven months too late."

Too late. Too late. Too late.

The refrain had drifted through his mind last night as he'd stood there in town making conversation with Donovan Delaney. It had stayed while he'd dropped his daughter off at home. Stayed as he'd headed to his father's guest house, the place he'd called home since his marriage to Lara had broken up and she and Belle had moved to an older home that had "potential."

He was almost home when he'd realized he was angry, angry for the past all over again. This time, though, the emotion was directed at himself and his father, instead of Sophie. If he'd had more backbone back then, if he'd been big enough to thumb his nose at the people who would have made fun of him for squiring Sophie Delaney around, things might have been different.

He'd muttered a low curse. He wasn't naive enough to believe he and Sophie could have actually made a go of it, but he was smart enough to realize that somehow, his brief relationship with her had been a pivotal time in his life. With her behind him, believing in him, he might have found the courage to stand up to his dad and follow his heart years sooner than he had.

But *had* she believed in him? Or had that been an act, a lie, just as her confession of love had been? He didn't know, but seeing Sophie had become imperative, even if it meant drumming up the lame excuse of offering help for Donovan.

Seeing her hadn't helped. He'd gained no brilliant insight to the past—except that she still held hard feelings for the way he'd dropped her. If the look in her eyes was anything to go by, she despised him.

The telephone rang. Reed swore and snatched it up, his link to the past broken. And all the while he talked, the refrain echoed through his mind.

Too late. Too late… Too late?

Chapter Five

It was midmorning before Sophie and Cassidy got around to driving into town. Fontaine's, the independently owned grocery store where Ruby Delaney had shopped, now carried the logo of a popular chain grocery, but when they went inside, Mr. Fontaine was still there, a bit older and grayer than when Sophie had seen him last, but with his toothy smile still in place.

As he had when she was a child, Frank Fontaine made it a point to chat to everyone who came through the doors. Sophie and Cassidy were no exception. He spoke to her, recognized who she was and commented on how long it had been since he'd seen her. He wished Donovan luck on his new endeavor, asked what she was doing these days, told her he was sorry about her mama's—and her husband's—death and told her how pretty Cassidy was. His concern and interest was genuine, one of the things she remembered loving about small-town living.

Sophie and Cassidy moved slowly down the aisles, referring often to their list and picking up all the grocery items they thought Donovan might need to set up housekeeping, as well as buying ahead for a few days' meals.

They were debating over the ease of putting a pork loin on the smoker as opposed to a roast in the crock pot when someone said, "Hi, Cassidy!"

Sophie and Cassidy turned toward the youthful voice. A dark-haired pixyish looking girl of eleven or twelve stood smiling at them, a bag of cat food clutched in her arms.

"Belle! Hi! How are you?" Cassidy said, smiling at the sprite in obvious pleasure.

"Fine. Piewacket was out of food, so Mom had to bring me to the store."

"Piewacket? That's a neat name for a cat."

"It's from a really old movie," the younger girl said. "Some blond woman is supposed to be a witch—but a good one—and her cat's name is Piewacket. *My* Piewacket is just a stray who showed up one day, but I think he adopted me."

"Cats do that," Cassidy said.

Sophie listened to the exchange, remembering Donovan saying that Reed had been with his daughter at the Dairy Delight the night before. Belle must be Lara's and Reed's daughter. Reed's *other* daughter, Sophie amended. She glanced over her shoulder and squelched a sudden, irrational panic at the thought of running into Reed, then remembered that the girl had said her mother brought her to the store.

Belle turned to Sophie, shifted the bag and extended her small hand. "You must be Cassidy's mom. I'm Belle Hardisty. Actually, it's Isabelle, after my mom's great-aunt, Isabelle Duncan."

"Hello, Belle," Sophie said, thinking that while there was much of Reed in Belle, there was also much of Lara.

"It's nice to meet you," Belle said. "Will you be staying in Lewiston long?"

"We'll be here for a couple of weeks," Sophie said, impressed with the girl's manners. "We're helping my brother get moved."

"That would be Donovan," Belle said with a smile.

"Mr. Delaney to you, young lady."

The correction came from a pleasant feminine voice somewhere behind Sophie. She turned and saw Lara Hardisty pushing a grocery buggy toward them, a stern expression on her face. Satisfied that she'd put Belle in her place, Lara turned to Sophie with a smile.

"Hello, Sophie," she said in a soft voice that conjured up images of mint juleps, hoop skirts and moss-draped oak trees.

Sophie remembered that the housekeeper who had lived with the Graysons until some time after their mother died had been from Savannah. "Hello, Lara. It's been a long time."

"Yes," Lara agreed. "It has."

Without bothering with small talk about how they'd both been the past seventeen years, Sophie said, "I just met Belle. She's delightful."

Belle made a face at being dubbed delightful, and Cassidy laughed.

Lara turned to Cassidy and extended her hand.

"You must be Cassidy. You're all I've heard about since last night. I'm Lara Hardisty."

"Nice to meet you," Cassidy said, her face bright with embarrassment at being the topic of any conversation, even that of a preteen girl.

"You, too." Lara turned to Sophie and asked the same question her daughter had asked before. "Will you be in town long?"

"I guess you heard that Donovan is moving back," Sophie said, wondering how Lara was taking the news. Uh-oh! Was it her imagination, or did Lara's full lips tighten the slightest bit?

"I do recall Wes saying something about that," Lara said, her voice still pleasant.

"Cassidy and I came to help him move," Sophie said. "We'll be here a couple of weeks." *If I can stand the stress of worrying about running into your ex-husband every time I come to town.*

"Good. You haven't been back often enough since you left. Aunt Isabelle said your mother missed you terribly."

"I know," Sophie said. "We got involved with our lives, you know? And time has a way of slipping by—not that that's an acceptable excuse."

"I understand. And it slips by much faster the older I get," Lara said in a dry tone. "What are you doing these days?"

"I'm a family counselor. I have my own practice."

"That's right," she said nodding. "I believe Reed mentioned something about that."

Reed mentioned it? That was a startling bit of news. Why would he bother to keep up with her and what she was doing? "What about you?" Sophie asked, hoping to steer the conversation away from herself.

"I'm the principal at the high school." Lara smiled. "It was close, but I got the position in spite of the good-old-boy mentality around here. Don't think that wasn't a nine-day wonder."

Sophie thought of all the people who'd been on the school board when she was young. Though the faces had changed, the attitudes were no doubt the same. "I imagine so."

"Mom, don't forget the washing machine repairman is supposed to be at the house in ten minutes," Belle reminded her.

Lara glanced at her watch. "Good grief! You're right. I've got to run. It's been good seeing you." The expression in her eyes grew serious. "I mean that, Sophie."

"Thanks."

"Belle, honey, put your cat food in the buggy and let's go check out."

"Mom, can Cassidy come over and go swimming this afternoon?" Belle asked.

Sophie's heart sank. The last thing she needed was for Cassidy and Belle to strike up a friendship. "Thanks for asking, Belle," she hedged, "but we have a lot to do, and I don't want her to impose."

"Impose? Don't be silly," Lara said. "It would be a help to me. Belle's best friend has gone to her grandparents' for two weeks, and she's at loose ends. Cassidy would be company for her—if she doesn't mind hanging out with a twelve-year old."

"Pleeease," Belle begged.

Sophie looked at Cassidy who said, "I wouldn't mind swimming for a while."

Sophie sighed. She was outnumbered. "All right, then, but just for a couple of hours."

They finalized the plans, and Lara and Belle headed for the checkout lane. Even though it was against her better judgment, Sophie would let Cassidy go. As slim as it was, she worried about the chance that somehow Cassidy would find out the truth of her paternity, but with any luck at all, it wouldn't be today.

"This is a great pool," Cassidy said, heaving herself up onto the cool deck where Belle lay on her stomach, resting her cheek on her arms while she'd watched Cassidy swim laps.

"It's a lot of fun when there's someone to swim with," Belle said. "Thanks for coming over and keeping me company. I know you'd rather hang out with someone your own age."

"That's not necessarily true," Cassidy said, reaching for a towel. "You seem older than twelve."

"Mom says I'm an old soul," Belle quipped with a grimace. "Whatever that means."

"That you act older than you are, I think," Cassidy said, scrubbing the fluffy lime-green towel over her head.

Belle perked up and smiled. "Oh. I'm like, mature for my age?"

"Yeah. And maybe wise about things most kids aren't." Cassidy spread out her towel and stretched out on her back beside her new friend, using her forearm for a pillow.

"Are your parents divorced?" Belle asked.

A cloud drifted across the sunshine of Cassidy's afternoon. She shook her head. "My dad died a couple of years ago."

Compassion darkened Belle's eyes. "I'm sorry. Do you miss him?"

"Yeah. A lot. He was a great dad, and he and Mom were crazy about each other."

Belle propped her chin up on her palm and regarded Cassidy with a serious expression. "How could you tell?"

"I don't know," Cassidy said. "It was just something about the way they looked at each other. They talked a lot and laughed a lot, and they were always kissing and touching and stuff. You know."

Belle sighed. After a moment she said, "My mom and dad weren't like yours. Before they got a divorce, I mean. I was only six, but I can remember how they never laughed or anything. It's funny, but they seem a lot happier since they split up."

Though Cassidy herself was pretty mature for her age, Belle was getting into some heavy issues, and Cassidy wasn't sure she could find the right explanations for topics she had no experience with. Still, it seemed imperative that she try. She sat up and wrapped her arms around her updrawn knees, turning to Belle with a serious expression.

"Sometimes people just fall out of love, Belle, and it's no one's fault. If they're happier now, maybe the divorce wasn't such a bad thing."

Belle thought about that. "Maybe. They do get along great now. I mean, they never argue anymore, and they seem to *like* each other. Do you know what I mean?"

Cassidy nodded.

"Some of the kids at school whose parents are divorced are always talking about how their moms and dads fight over everything."

"Then count your blessings," Cassidy told her. She recalled her conversation with her mother that morning. "Would it bother you if your dad got married again?"

"No," Belle said with a shake of her head. "Not if he really loved the other woman. What about you?"

"No," Cassidy said. "Not if he was a good guy...."

Wes Grayson, who was taking a day off to devote to a painting he'd started before a particularly nasty divorce case began, stood at the French doors in his sister's kitchen, sipping on a glass of iced tea while she took a phone call, observing the two girls at the pool. His niece had climbed out a few minutes earlier, and he watched as the older girl jumped up onto the edge of the pool and reached for a towel. She swiped the moisture from an incredible body, spread the bright lime-green rectangle next to Belle's bright orange towel and lay down beside her. They might have been sisters, with their dark hair and long legs.

Belle said something, something serious, if the expression on her face was any indication. After a moment or two of conversation, the older girl sat up and hugged her knees to her chest, turning to face Belle, a solemn expression on her own face. Shock drove the air from Wes's lungs.

Naturally observant and blessed with an artist's ability to see the relationship of curves and angles as well as the affinity of different hues and lights and darks, it was clear to Wes that the girls' resemblance went beyond hair color and long legs. Lured by a desire to be sure, he opened the door and stepped out onto the porch. The likeness was even more obvious there. Their profiles were exactly the same, from the shape of their foreheads and the slant of their noses, right down to their pointed chins. He did a little quick calculating.

Reed, old buddy, what the heck have you been up to?

"Sorry about that."

Lara's cheerful voice preceded her as she stepped out onto the porch. Wes pushed his startling discovery to the back of his mind.

"That was Chloe Martin wanting to know if she and I can carpool to dance class this summer."

"I'd carpool with Chloe anywhere," Wes drawled.

Lara laughed. "She's a looker all right and available since her divorce came through, but I know you. That nonstop chatter of hers would drive you crazy inside an hour."

"You're right," Wes said. "It's hard to find a woman who understands that there can be communication in silence." He cocked his head toward the pool. "Who's that with Belle? I can't place her."

"Cassidy Carlisle."

"And who is Cassidy Carlisle?" he asked, taking a long pull from his glass of tea.

"Sophie Carlisle—Sophie Delaney's—daughter."

"Sophie Delaney?"

The pieces of the puzzle fell into place. Wes's mouth tightened. He recalled a time seventeen years earlier when he and Reed had asked out Sophie and her cousin. Reed and Sophie saw each other a few times, then when her dad was killed, she left town. When she came back for her brother's trial, she was married and clearly pregnant. Reed was more than a little upset.

Wes had wondered at his friend's anger at the time, and now it made a bit more sense. Reed might not have wanted the ties of marriage, but he must have still cared enough for Sophie that the idea of her taking up with a stranger so soon had rankled.

For his part, Justine Sutton had been all and more that Wes had hoped she'd be. But he didn't want to think about Justine. She was on his mind far too often, especially lately. He turned his attention from his sister back to the girls lounging by the pool.

"Maybe that's why she looks familiar."

"Probably."

"What's she doing here? Isn't she a little old to be hanging out with Belle?"

Lara looked out at the two girls, who were still oblivious to the fact that they were being discussed. "Swimming, obviously, and yes, she's a little old for Belle, but since she's only visiting for a couple of weeks I couldn't see any harm in letting her come over and swim. Heather is out of town for a week or so."

"How did Belle and Cassidy meet?"

Lara tucked back a strand of hair that had worked its way loose from the scrunchie. "Belle was with her dad last night at the Dairy Delight. Donovan Delaney and Cassidy came in as they were leaving."

Wes wondered if the bitter note he heard in his sister's voice was real or imagined. Imagined, surely. There was no reason for her to be bitter, unless Sophie was a reminder that Reed had once dated the other woman in secret. But if it was as secret as it seemed to be, how would she know? Had Reed confessed?

"Belle really took a shine to Cassidy," Lara said. "All I heard last night was how pretty Cassidy was, how sweet, how friendly. Then, this morning, we went to buy cat food, and who should we run into but Cassidy and Sophie? Belle was thrilled and asked Cassidy over. It seemed churlish to refuse, even though I never knew Sophie all that well.''

Definitely a secret. "Always the proper one, aren't you, little sister?''

"Someone has to be, brother, dear,'' she said. She reached out and brushed back a lock of his dark hair, hair that was at least two forgotten haircuts too long. "And it certainly isn't going to be you. You need a haircut, not to mention a shave. I can't believe you go to work looking so…casual,'' she said, for lack of a better word. Unlike Reed, who favored thousand-dollar suits for work, Wes preferred jeans and T-shirts. When he really got dressed up, he deigned to don khaki slacks and a golf shirt.

Now, he pretended a wounded grimace. "Cut to the bone,'' he said, but he smiled. "I keep meaning to get a haircut, but I've been really busy since Chicago.''

As soon as he said it, he wished he hadn't. He didn't want to talk about Chicago. The meeting with the art gallery there had been successful and the dealer was interested in giving him a one-man show when he got enough pieces ready. It was Wes's dream to give up law and devote his life to painting, but he couldn't, in good conscience, abandon Reed or their practice, and until recently his work hadn't found the acceptance he'd hoped for. Now, even though he seemed to have found a sponsor, none of the pictures he'd started since he came back from Chicago were shaping up the way he would like.

On a personal level, Chicago had been a disaster.

Justine Sutton had been in town for a concert, and, like a fool, unable to help himself he'd not only gone to hear her sing but had gone backstage to say hello. She'd been surprised, but when he asked her up to his room for a couple of drinks and to talk about old times and old friends, she'd agreed. After a few drinks Wes forgot how badly she'd hurt him and kissed her. She'd kissed him back, and the flame had turned into a raging firestorm, just as he'd known it would. He'd awakened the next morning a headache tap-dancing against his skull, anger at himself churning in his stomach. How many times did a woman have to make a fool of him before he learned his lesson?

"Chicago was really good then?" Lara asked, unaware of the frustration churning inside him.

"Yeah," Wes said, a wry twist to his lips. "Really good."

"I'm proud for you. Dad would be, too."

Wes cocked an eyebrow at his sister. "I doubt that."

Phil Grayson had never been proud of anything Wes had done, and he'd hated the idea of his son taking up a "sissy" occupation like painting. So Wes had become a lawyer, teaming up with Reed in a general practice. Even though it wasn't his career of choice, he was a damn good attorney. But frustration had eaten away at him for years, and he'd begun to drink too much. It had taken less than a year after his father's death for Wes to donate his Brooks Brothers suits to the Salvation Army and start painting again in earnest. He still did his share of work for the partnership, but chose to work at home whenever possible.

"Did you get any commissions from Chicago?"

"A couple." Wes didn't want to talk about Chicago. "Look," he said pointing toward a border of red-tipped shrubs, "I think your photinias have a disease."

"I know," she said, her frown proving that his distraction worked. "It started with just one, then in a few weeks they all started looking bad. I need to call someone from Texarkana to come take a look and tell me what to do, if I don't want to lose them all."

"Shame on you, Lara. Don't you believe in the town motto of supporting our local economy? Donovan Delaney is back and starting up a new landscape business. Why don't you call him? I understand he's a whiz."

"Donovan Delaney?" Lara said, as if the very idea were foreign.

"Reed tells me that anyone who was anyone in Baton Rouge used Delaney to landscape his yard."

"Really?"

"Really. They say he was the person who took the company he worked for to the top, so he decided to try it on his own." There was a faraway expression in Lara's eyes, something almost…wistful, Wes thought.

"So he made something of himself in spite of everything," she said in a barely audible voice.

"Only in America," Wes quipped.

His sarcasm broke whatever spell was binding her. She reached for Wes's glass. "More tea?"

"Sure. Why not? Are you going to the festival?" he called after her.

Lara slipped through the door and gave him a look that asked if he was crazy. "How can you live in Lewiston and not go to the festival?"

"Easy. I haven't been in years," he said.

"You're a hermit. Or would like to be."

"I'm not a hermit. I just like my privacy."

Lara smiled and disappeared into the kitchen. From across the street Wes heard a car door slam shut, a dog barking, children laughing. Nostalgia washed over him. What would it be like to be that carefree? That happy? He didn't recall a time his own life hadn't been complicated, though he was sure there was such a time. Maybe before his mother died.

Suddenly a stranger's head appeared over the top of the backyard fence. The man spoke to the girls. Wes pushed himself away from the porch post. It was broad daylight, and the girls, who were behind a locked fence, didn't appear to be alarmed, but he decided to check out the newcomer, anyway.

The man was big and muscular and looked as if his nose had been broken a time or two. The faint line of an old scar angled across the left side of his chin. He glanced at Wes as he neared the pool area, showing no signs of fear or intimidation.

"Hi, Uncle Wes!" Belle said. "This—"

"Is there something I can do for you?" Wes asked, ignoring his niece's greeting.

The stranger grinned. "Yeah," he said in a husky voice. "I want to commission you to paint a naked lady for my den."

Something about the Sam Elliot-like voice was familiar, even though Wes hadn't heard it in years. Recognition came in a rush. Donovan Delaney.

"Sounds like your kind of picture," Wes said, smiling back. "How are you, Donovan?"

"Never better," Delaney said with another slow grin. Something about the tone of his voice told Wes he meant it. "That's great." He started to hold out his hand in greeting and realized the fence was too high. "I'd let you in, but I don't have the key."

"No problem. I just came to pick up Cassidy." He glanced at his niece. "Run and get your stuff together, kiddo. Your mom'll have my hide if I'm gone too long."

"No kidding," Cassidy said. "When she's remodeling, she's a woman with a mission. C'mon, Belle."

The two men watched the girls gather their towels and head for the back door.

"So you're fixing up the old home place, huh?" Wes asked, stuffing his hands into the back pockets of his khaki shorts.

"Yeah. It needs a major overhaul. Sophie was in the middle of painting the bedroom, and since—according to her—I was just standing around outside staring at things, I was elected to come. What she didn't realize is that I was designing in my mind."

Wes laughed. Though he and Donovan Delaney had both grown up in the same town and had graduated the same year, they'd never hung out together, coming as they had from different stratas of Lewiston society. Still, it was inevitable that their paths crossed.

Wes had learned that, despite his background, Delaney was a pretty decent guy. Isabelle Duncan had told him recently that the Delaney children could thank their mother for that. The times they had attended the same functions, Wes had enjoyed Delaney's company.

"I know what you mean," he said. "I do some of my best painting staring off into space. Are you about to get settled in?"

"I wish," Donovan said with a shake of his head.

"According to Sophie it may take till this time next year for us to get the place in shape."

Wes laughed. "Yeah. Lara's been working on this house ever since she and Reed split up, and it still isn't finished."

Donovan looked around the yard, his interest apparent. "Nice place, but I'd have figured Lara for something brand-spanking-new."

"Actually, she likes old things. Says there's something about antiques and old stuff that helps ground you in the past."

"Her photinia has a fungus."

"Yeah, I—"

"Wes just told me that," Lara said in a cool voice from behind them.

Wes turned, and Donovan, still on the other side of the fence, swiveled his head toward her. Lara stood a few feet away, her hands clasping a frosty glass of mint-sprigged tea. She gave the appearance of nonchalance, but Wes had the feeling she was anything but relaxed.

"By the way," she said, in a challenging tone that puzzled him even more, "did you grow an extra two feet since you've been gone, or do you walk around on stilts?"

"Pardon?" Donovan replied.

"How can you see over a six-foot-high fence?"

Donovan smiled an easy smile that didn't reach his eyes. "I'm standing on a rotting stump. You should have had it ground down before you put up the fence. It's full of termites."

"I should have done a lot of things differently."

"Yeah," Donovan said with a nod. "Shouldn't we all?"

As Wes listened, he had the strangest feeling they weren't talking about stumps at all.

"I suppose you've come for Cassidy," Lara said.

"Yeah. Sophie was busy."

"Use the front door next time."

Wes almost recoiled in shock at his sister's rudeness. He saw nothing in Donovan's manner to cause her to be so short, and it wasn't like her to take an instant dislike to someone.

Donovan's gaze—an insolent gaze, Wes thought—raked Lara from head to toe.

"I'm not sure there'll be a next time," Donovan said.

"It's extremely doubtful."

"Why's that?" Wes asked the question before he could stop himself. Both Lara and Donovan looked at him as if they just realized he was there.

Clearly flustered, Lara's face turned red. She was saved from answering by the return of the two girls.

"I think we got all Cassidy's stuff," Belle said.

"If you didn't, we can drop it off," Lara said, bemusement replacing the implacable expression on her face.

"Thanks for having me over, Ms. Hardisty," Cassidy said. "I had a nice time."

"You're welcome," Lara replied. She shoved the glass of tea at Wes, bent down, moved a rock at the edge of the gate and retrieved a key from a small plastic container. She unlocked the gate while the girls hugged. It was amazing how they'd taken to each other. Wes knew Belle was selective about who she hung out with, and she didn't suffer fools, no matter what their age.

Cassidy slipped through the gate. Donovan's head

disappeared from above the fence. With a wave they started toward the street, where his vehicle sat, already bearing magnetic signs that said Delaney's Nursery and Landscape Service.

He'd gone no more than three yards when he turned. "You know, Ms. Hardisty, if you let a condition go too long, it can spread. Next thing you know, it's killed out all the good."

Lara visibly stiffened. Again Wes had the feeling Donovan meant something other than what he actually said. What the hell was going on, anyway?

"What was that all about?"

Lara met her brother's questioning gaze with what she hoped was a noncommittal expression in her own. "What was what all about?"

"You were downright rude to that man."

"Was I?"

Wes stared at her. Lara scoured her mind for a suitable reply. "I guess he just caught me off guard, showing up like that out of the blue, looking over the fence. I mean, if you hadn't been here, I'd have been scared to death to walk out and see a strange man ogling the girls over the fence. And," she tacked on, "he did serve time in prison."

"C'mon, Lara. It couldn't have been that much of a shock. I mean, maybe for a second of two, but it isn't like he's a stranger, and you asked his niece over to swim. Didn't you think there was a fifty-fifty chance he might be the one to come pick her up?"

"I suppose," she said in a guarded voice.

"And besides, you weren't frightened. You were mad. Not to mention rude."

Knowing he was right, and furious at herself for

letting Donovan get to her in front of someone else no less, Lara whirled to face him. "And when did you become such a Donovan Delaney fan?"

"I'm not his fan," Wes said. "And I'm not his enemy. I think he's a guy who's had a hard time of it and somehow managed to turn out okay. All I want to know is what that was between the two of you."

"We were talking about my diseased shrubs."

"Like hell."

She hadn't thought he would buy it but she'd had to try. Now she summoned a cynical smile. "Wes, dear, you really should get out more. Intuitiveness about people used to be one of your strong suits. You've stayed in that cabin by the lake alone so long you've gotten out of touch. You don't read people very well anymore."

It was all Donovan could do to behave as if everything were normal as he and Cassidy got into the truck. He'd thought Sophie was crazy for letting Cassidy spend time with Belle Hardisty when there was the off chance that someone seeing them together might spot the resemblance to Reed that had fairly screamed at Donovan the night before. Sophie's rationale was that it would have been more awkward trying to find an acceptable excuse as to why she wouldn't let Cassidy go. At any rate, it was a done deal, and when Sophie had asked if he'd go pick Cassidy up, his first inclination was to refuse.

Curiosity had won out. As Reed no doubt had the night before, Donovan hadn't been able to resist the opportunity to see for himself how a mature Lara looked. Now he was wondering at the wisdom of that decision.

Seeing Lara in the flesh had made him acutely aware of how weak his memories had grown. She was still willowy and slender, with an elegance that had more to do with bone structure than the timelessness of her style of dressing. She'd aged beautifully, and he knew that, like a fine wine she'd only grown more perfect with age.

Her hair was thicker, a richer brown than he remembered, and her eyes weren't just dark, they were almost black. The people in south Louisiana would call them *les yeux noir,* black eyes. He'd forgotten the stubborn tilt of her chin and the delicate arch of her eyebrows. Forgotten just how sexy the shape of her mouth was and how just looking at it had turned him…until it happened again. Seeing her, knowing what he'd missed out on, had been bittersweet. Still, he wouldn't do things any differently, even now.

When he'd been arrested for shooting his father, Lara had wasted no time coming to see him. Knowing she was parading her feelings for him in front of the whole world had, in Donovan's mind, proved that the love she professed for him was real.

He'd wanted more than anything to have the jailer let her in, had needed to see her, to hear her voice, to touch her, more than he'd needed the air he breathed. But he was nothing if not a realist, and he knew that if he truly loved her he would let her go. The future they'd planned together could never be, and it wasn't fair for her to suffer embarrassment or shame for loving him, when she deserved so much more. So every time she'd come, he'd refused to see her. He'd returned her letters unopened.

Eventually she'd stopped coming, and Donovan, who'd often let his tears of grief fall long after the lights in the cell block had been turned out, had taken what small comfort he could from the knowledge that he'd done the right, the noble thing. As miserable as he was, he figured they would both get over it. He hadn't, but it hadn't taken Lara long to go back to Reed. He'd been angry when he'd first heard about their quick marriage, but he'd convinced himself she'd done it on the rebound, or even out of spite. Now there was Sophie's theory that the marriage was Rowland's and Phil's doing. No doubt bucking Rowland Hardisty in any way wouldn't be an easy task.

He sighed audibly, humbled by the brief meeting. Even though she was bound to have realized that what he'd done was for her own good, she hadn't forgiven him for rejecting her. Her attitude proved that. If he'd come back with any thoughts about trying to resurrect the feelings they'd shared—and as crazy as he knew it was, he had—he had his work cut out for him.

"You're awfully quiet," Cassidy said, the sound of her voice breaking into his thoughts.

"Just thinking about all there is to do," he lied. "It's almost overwhelming." He glanced over at her and smiled. "Did you have a good time?"

"Yeah." The word held more than a hint of surprise. "I know she's a lot younger and everything, but for some reason Belle and I really hit it off. Almost like we're—I don't know—bound together some way. Do you know what I mean?"

Donovan's heart felt as if it were being squeezed by a giant fist. He'd heard about the uncanny bond between twins who had been separated at birth. Was it possible that all siblings felt some tug of recognition?

He didn't know, but he needed to tell Sophie how Cassidy felt. There was a potential heartbreak brewing here, and all of them had had more than their share of that.

Chapter Six

"I can't believe we're actually going to the Wood-cutters' Festival," Donovan said a week later. "It isn't as if there's nothing to do around here."

"There's plenty to do," Sophie said, reaching for her sunglasses. "But we've done a lot, too. We deserve a break. Especially Cassidy."

Blake Meriweather and his crew of four had shown up soon after Donovan called them. They had knocked down a couple of walls to enlarge the living room and built another to add a second bathroom. They had installed some oak cabinets in the kitchen while the plumber did his job and, in a matter of days, they'd finished the inside work. Then they'd started putting up the framing for the greenhouses so Donovan could start his cuttings and seedlings in the fall and be ready to ship out plants the following spring. Donovan was putting in the watering system himself.

Sophie and Cassidy had cleaned up the mess, painted and stripped the old wax off the floors, revealing pine boards in surprisingly good condition. Cassidy, ever the perfectionist, had proved remarkable with a paintbrush and alkyd paint, a task neither Donovan nor Sophie wanted any part of. They'd all worked hard, and they deserved a day off, even if they were just going to the Woodcutters' Festival.

"It'll be fun," Sophie said, trying to coax Donovan into a better mood. "Besides, Cassidy has made five hundred flyers on the computer for you to pass out. It'll be a good opportunity for you to let people know you're here and will be ready for business by fall."

"I imagine they're waiting with bated breath," Donovan said.

"Let's be a little more positive, please," Sophie told him.

"I'll try." A reluctant smile curved Donovan's mouth. "So if I go to this shindig, do I get to eat all the junk food I want?"

"Why, of course you do," Sophie said, patting his arm in a motherly fashion. "And you can drink a dozen colas, too, if you want—as long as you smile nicely when you hand out the flyers."

"Cotton candy?"

"Cotton candy."

"Gee, thanks, Mom."

Sophie winked at Cassidy. "Promise your Uncle Donovan a Twinkie and he'll be your slave for life."

Donovan grinned, Cassidy laughed and Sophie thought how good it felt to be at a point where teasing and laughter was part of their lives once again. There'd been too many solemn, somber days since Jake died. This trip had been good for that reason, she decided, even if she did spend far too much time thinking about Reed Hardisty. If she could only make it through another week or so without running into him, she'd be home-free.

The festival was set up at the city park. There was a small midway with rides for the younger children and plenty of games to sucker the older ones out of their money. There was a section of arts and crafts and businesses selling samples of their wares. The cheerleaders had a booth selling tickets for a raffle, the arts council was signing kids up for a summer arts workshop, and the sheriff's department was finger-printing children, as a matter of precaution.

A five-mile run, softball games and a golf tourna-ment were planned in conjunction with the festivities, and a peewee rodeo was planned for the fairgrounds that night. In keeping with the festival name, there were stump-cutting and log-splitting competitions. After the sun went down, there would be a fireworks display to finish out the day.

To Donovan's delight, there were several vendors selling snow cones, lemonade, turkey legs, cotton candy and funnel cakes. He was, he told Cassidy with a gleam in his eyes, a happy man. Sophie didn't be-lieve that for one moment. Content, maybe, but not truly happy. In fact, he'd been unusually quiet ever since the day he'd picked Cassidy up at the Hardistys. She figured he was dealing with seeing Lara in his own way.

The park was packed; everyone was trying to beat the heat that would settle over the day as the sun climbed higher in the cloudless summer sky. Dono-van, Sophie and Cassidy wended their way through the crowd, trying their hand at several games, picking up craft items that appealed to them and having a huge pancake-and-sausage breakfast sponsored by the Lions Club.

Donovan spotted Isabelle Duncan in a floral dress straight from the forties, browsing through the used books being sold by the literacy council. Saying that he needed to introduce Cassidy to his benefactor and thank her for helping push through his loan, he and Cassidy left Sophie alone to pass out the fliers.

She was surprised at the interest shown in Donovan's new undertaking. With gardening becoming more popular, even in urban areas, and with a rising interest in extending living space outdoors, the younger couples, who probably weren't aware of Donovan's past, seemed thrilled that there would be a place nearby to fill their gardening needs. The only resistance they'd encountered came from the older people, who remembered seeing Donovan on trial for his father's murder and were worried about having an ex-convict in their midst.

On her way to get something to drink, Sophie paused to listen to the spiel of a local artisan who crafted exquisite pieces from different kinds of wood. While he spoke with a couple who were considering the purchase of an inlaid cedar chest, Sophie admired a gorgeous inlaid box.

"Fantastic, isn't it?"

The words were innocent enough, but the low timbre of the voice sent a shiver of awareness down her spine. She bit back a gasp and set down the box before she dropped it. Reed. Hoping she could hide the nervousness that had settled in her stomach like a covey of skittish quail, she turned to look over her shoulder.

"He's very talented," Sophie said, wishing she was wearing something besides shorts and a T-shirt emblazoned with Donovan's logo and the words Delaney Landscaping and Nursery.

"I didn't expect to see you here," Reed said.

I was hoping I wouldn't see you. Sophie picked up a vase, more to prove her nonchalance than because she was interested in it. "We all needed a break. We've had our noses to the grindstone for a week."

"Did the construction crew I recommended work out okay?" Reed asked, moving to her side so she had to look at him. It was hard not to. He was breathtaking in khaki slacks and a golf shirt of soft sage-green with the morning sun tipping his brown hair with gold, an easy smile playing with his beautifully shaped lips. Lips that had once driven her crazy with need.

Stop it, Sophie! It was only sex, and not even very good sex at that! They'd been so innocent—or she had, at least. But even if Reed had been the most sophisticated lover on earth, there was something about the back seat of a car that reduced the whole experience to awkward absurdity. No. Not absurd. They'd been too intense to be considered absurd. They'd been trying so hard to prove...what? In her case that she loved him. Or thought she did.

She sneaked a glance at him from the corner of her eye, caught him looking at her and felt her insides quiver with a delicious longing. Somehow she knew he wouldn't be awkward now, even in the back seat of a car....

"Sophie?"

The sound of his voice pulled her attention back to him. "Yes?"

"I asked about Meriweather."

"Oh, he was great," she said brightly, hoping he couldn't see the emotions that had surfaced along with her memories. "He did an excellent job, in fact. They've already finished the house and started framing up the greenhouses."

"Good."

"Hi, there." The vendor had finished his sale and was pocketing a fistful of money. Sensing he had a couple more potential buyers hooked, he smiled at Reed. "That vase your lady is looking at is a particular favorite of mine."

His lady? Feeling the unaccustomed heat of another blush burning her cheeks, Sophie slanted a glance at Reed, who gave a slight, unobtrusive shrug. Obviously, the man wasn't from Lewiston, or he'd know better. She pretended interest in the vase, whose wood grain resembled the veining in marble.

"I like the long throat of the vase," the vendor said. "I've always though long necks were classy, whether they were on a vase, a swan or a woman. Take your missus, here. She's a tiny little thing, but she's still got that elegant neck—don't you think?"

Reed turned to Sophie and let his gaze move over her face. The intensity in his eyes made her uncomfortable, and he knew it, but he made a leisurely survey of her eyes and her mouth before letting his gaze dip to her neck and beyond, to the swell of her breasts beneath the T-shirt.

"I think she's classy all over," Reed said in a husky voice.

Sophie's cheeks burned hotter.

"Touch it," the man urged. "You won't find wood any smoother anywhere."

Reed reached out and slid his hand down the neck of the vase Sophie was holding, to the swell of the bowl, his hand cupping the smooth roundness the way it had once cupped her breast. "Like satin," he agreed.

Before Sophie realized what he was about to do, he lifted the same hand to her cheek. She sucked in a startled breath. There was a challenge in his eyes as his knuckles grazed her cheekbone and drifted down to the curve of her jaw. *Make me stop,* the look seemed to say. *Dare you.*

But of course she didn't. Couldn't. All she could do was stand there with her nerve endings sizzling, her heart beating like that of a frightened bird. Then, as he'd done the vase, he cupped her cheek in his palm in a brief, featherlight caress. He turned to the vendor. "The vase is smooth, no doubt about it, but it can't hold a candle to her skin."

The man laughed and winked at Sophie. "He doesn't want to sleep on the couch tonight, does he?"

Unable to think of a witty reply or some word to refute his assumption that they were married, Sophie just shook her head.

"How 'bout it, mister? Want me to wrap it up for you? It'd make a nice gift for your lady."

Reed turned to Sophie, a teasing glint in his golden-brown eyes. Funny. She didn't remember him having a sense of humor seventeen years ago. "What about it, honey? Should we take it home?" he asked, playing along.

"Do what you want," she said.

"Do you like it?"

"Yes, but—"

"Then we'll take it," Reed said to the man. "How much?"

Sophie wandered to the next booth while he paid the man and tucked the brown-paper-wrapped vase under his arm. When he caught up to her, he held out the package. "Here."

Her mouth fell open with astonishment. "I can't take that."

"But you said you liked it."

"I do, but I can't take a gift from you, Reed."

"Why?"

Her eyes widened, and she glanced around to see if anyone was listening. "Why? You know why."

"Because I was a jerk seventeen years ago, or because I was the first man you had sex with?"

Sophie was so stunned by his ability to talk with such frankness about something she could hardly bear to think about, she did the only thing she could: she walked away. As he had the night he'd come to the house, he caught her arm, forcing her to turn and face him.

"It happened, Sophie," he said, an earnest expression in his eyes. "We can't change it. Maybe I didn't handle things right, but I was under a lot guilt that I didn't know how to deal with."

Guilt? She hoped so. Even though she knew she should have forgiven him long ago, she knew deep in her heart that she hadn't. She'd paid the price for her mistake, and he had gotten off scot-free. She hoped he was still *consumed* with guilt for abandoning her and his baby. She hoped it left him sleepless night after night the way her heartbreak had her.

"What do you want from me, Reed?" she said in

a low, angry voice. "Forgiveness? I'm sorry. I can't quite manage that. As for your guilt, why don't you find yourself a good counselor and see if you can't come to terms with it?" She pulled her arm free. "I have to go."

She was a little surprised that he let her, but she knew he had too much class to force a confrontation. She hurried away, scanning the throng, searching for Donovan and Cassidy. She gasped in shock when her gaze skimmed over the figure of her mother. No. On closer inspection, she realized that the woman she was looking at was her aunt, who looked incredibly old and tired, even though she was only fifty-five. Opal was much grayer than Ruby Delaney had been when she died and thin to the point of emaciation. Ruby had grown plump in her later years, but it was a pleasing plumpness that had given her an air of vigor and health, albeit a false one.

Hoping Reed wouldn't follow, Sophie made a beeline for her aunt. She gave Opal Malone a hug and apologized for not stopping by to visit yet, using the unending work at Donovan's as her excuse.

"I'm glad he's come home," Opal said, scanning the flyer Sophie handed her.

"I hope it's the right thing to do," Sophie said, still unconvinced.

"Following your dream is always the right thing, Sophia. Donovan's a good man. Folks will come around."

Sophie sighed. "I hope so."

Opal folded the flyer and put it in her purse. "Have you heard from Justine lately?"

"Actually, I spoke with her a few days before we came up here."

"How is she? I haven't talked to her in a month of Sundays." An interest bordering on hunger shone in Opal Malone's eyes.

What should she say? Sophie wondered. It wasn't her place to tell her aunt that her oldest daughter was pregnant. "She seemed fine," she hedged. "You know Justine. She stays so busy that she's exhausted all the time. And now that her singing career is going so well—"

"You don't have to make excuses," Opal said in a tone that said she'd long ago given up justifying why Justine didn't keep in touch more often. "We aren't close and haven't been in a long time. I don't suppose she'll ever forgive me."

Sophie recalled Justine saying the same thing. What did they mean? What could her aunt have done to cause such a rift between herself and her daughter?

"What on earth could she possibly have to forgive you for?" Sophie queried, putting her thoughts into words as she slid an arm around her aunt's thin shoulders. The fragility of the bones beneath Opal's cotton blouse alarmed Sophie.

"Something that happened a long time ago," Opal said, reaching up to clasp Sophie's hand. "Don't fret about it, honey. I understand why she feels the way she does."

"Do you want to talk about it?"

"No," Opal said. "I don't think Justine would appreciate me talking about it."

More confused than ever, Sophie gave her aunt's shoulders a light squeeze. "So what about you? Are you all right?"

Opal pulled away and turned to face her. "Actually, I'm not." She took a deep breath and said, "I was diagnosed with cancer a few weeks ago. It's…pretty far advanced, so I've decided not to waste my time with chemotherapy. There's no sense putting Molly through that.''

Molly, who was only two years older than Cassidy, was Justine's youngest sister, the only child left at home. Sophie's eyes filled with tears. ''Oh, Aunt Opal! I'm so sorry.''

Opal shrugged. ''It happens. I worry about leaving Molly alone. She seems so much younger than Justine did at eighteen. But I own the house free and clear, and I have a small insurance policy that will get her partway through college.'' She shrugged. ''I thought that maybe since Justine's singing career is taking off she'd help.''

''Of course she will. We all will. You know Molly can call on any of us at any time.''

Opal reached for Sophie's hand and squeezed. There were tears in her eyes. ''You're so much like your mama.''

Sophie smiled. ''I take that as a compliment.''

''We had so many dreams,'' Opal said, a faraway look in her eyes. ''She deserved better than Hutch Delaney.'' She fixed Sophie with a questioning glance. ''Did she ever talk about Micah Lawrence?''

Sophie frowned. ''Never. Why?''

''He was her real love. But when his family moved away and Hutch started coming around, she let him convince her that he could make her happy.''

''Mama was in love with Sheriff Lawrence?'' Sophie said, unable to hide her surprise.

Opal nodded.

''I can't believe it. But as for Dad making her

happy, I think he did,'' Sophie said in her father's defense. ''Until his drinking started.''

''She was content,'' Opal said. ''But not really happy, just the way I was with both my husbands.'' She gave a short laugh. ''No, forget that. I wasn't happy or content with Gene.'' She shook her head. ''Now there was a sorry excuse for a human being.''

Sophie thought it best not to say anything, even though she agreed with her aunt 100 percent. Gene Malone had left his wife with three children to care for on a waitress's salary. Molly hadn't even been six. Justine, who had already been gone from home for five years when her stepfather abandoned the rest of his family, was spared that particular trauma.

''If there's one thing I've learned through the years, Sophia,'' Opal said, ''it's not to settle for second best. Go for whatever it is your heart wants with everything you have. If you don't get it, at least you know you gave it your best shot.''

Sophie understood what her aunt was saying. It had been the theory behind her own struggle to become a psychologist, even with the odds stacked against her. In the end, it had paid off.

Opal Malone soon took her leave, telling Sophie to bring Cassidy over for a visit one day before they left for Baton Rouge, Sophie promising she would.

''She looks terrible, doesn't she?'' Donovan said, coming to a halt beside Sophie as their aunt disappeared in the crowd.

''She has cancer.''

''Damn,'' Donovan said. ''Is it bad?''

''Bad enough she's refused chemotherapy. I thinks she wants whatever is left of her life to be quality time, not spent miserable and sick.''

"Sounds like a good idea, if they haven't given her any hope."

"Yeah."

They were both silent for a moment, thinking of the aunt they were soon to lose, their last link to Ruby Delaney and their youth. Finally Donovan said, "Well, on a happier note my guardian angel, better known as Isabelle Duncan, has asked me to go out and take a look at the high school. The grounds need some revamping. She wants me to submit a bid to the school board for some shrubs and things."

"That's great, Donovan," Sophie said with a pleased smile.

"It's a start," he agreed. He glanced around. "I've had about all the fun I can handle for one morning. Let's get out of here."

"I still have some flyers," Sophie said. "And I have no idea where Cassidy is."

"I spoke with the lady at the chamber of commerce booth. We can leave the extra flyers there. She'll see to it that they get put out around town. As for Cass, the last time I saw her, she and Jett were headed for the funnel cake concession," Donovan said. "He said he'd bring her home in an hour or so."

Jett Robbins was Blake Meriweather's nephew, who was working for his uncle for the summer. He had dark good looks, was a smooth talker and a hard worker. Cassidy had been smitten the moment she laid eyes on him, something that hadn't escaped Jett's notice. He flirted with her outrageously. Sophie wasn't sure if she admired his self-assurance or was fearful of it. She felt he might be just a bit too old and experienced for Cassidy.

"Jett?"

"Yes, Jett," Donovan said with extreme patience. "She's only going to be here for a another week, Sis, and he's only buying her a funnel cake. It isn't like she's marrying the guy."

"But he's so much older," Sophie said, her eyes panning the crowd with a worried expression.

"He's nineteen," Donovan consoled, "and he seems very responsible. I know he's a hard worker."

"I don't know…"

"I don't understand why you're so worried," Donovan said. "The kid is so much like me at that age, he could be mine."

"That's what worries me," Sophie said, knowing that he'd hit on the problem exactly.

"I turned out okay, didn't I?"

The pseudo-innocent expression in his eyes made Sophie laugh, and she felt her doubts melting like the snow cone someone had abandoned on one of the portable bleachers that had been set up for the entertainment. "You turned out better than okay. And you're right. I imagine Cassidy is sick to death of hanging around us all the time."

Donovan gave her a brief hug. "That's my girl."

"What's so interesting?" Lara Hardisty stood on tiptoe and craned her neck trying to get a glimpse of whatever it was Reed was staring at.

"Nothing."

"Oh," Lara said. "Sophie."

The tone of her voice implied much that wasn't said. He pinned her with a challenging look. "So I see Sophie over there. What of it?"

Lara held up her hands, palms out. "Hey, don't get huffy with me. All I said was, 'Oh, Sophie.'"

Reed's irritation died. Was he so transparent, then? "It was the way you said it."

"And how, pray tell, did I say it?"

"As if you thought I was interested in her."

"Well, you are."

"Don't be ridiculous."

"I saw you with her at the wood-carving exhibit. The way you were looking at her..." Lara's voice trailed away and she gave a slight shrug. "It only emphasized the point I've been trying to make for several weeks now."

"Which is?"

"That this notion of yours that the two of us should get back together because we like and respect each other and the sex was okay is ridiculous."

"I still think it's a good idea. As I recall, sometimes the sex was better than okay."

"Well, thanks for nothing, Mr. Hardisty," Lara said with a wry twist of her lips.

"You know what I meant," Reed growled, raking a hand through his hair.

"Yes, I do, but the point is sex between two people should be more than okay sometimes. It should be dynamite all the time."

"We're not teenagers anymore, Lara."

"No, but we aren't dead yet, either, which is why we were both considering your preposterous idea. We both like sex, and it's been a long time—for me, anyway. We both liked being married, which may be why we stuck it out as long as we did. I know you well enough to know that there haven't been that many women since we split up, that you don't like messy affairs and have been seeing Elissa Markham solely at your father's insistence. After a long dry spell even your likable ex starts looking good.''

Reed smiled. After sharing his life for eleven years, she knew him pretty well. He raised his eyebrows in query. ''So you did consider it?''

Lara blew out a troubled breath. ''Oh, yeah. I considered it. More seriously than you'll ever know. And if I hadn't seen...'' Her voice trailed away and a pensive expression filled her eyes.

''Seen what?'' Reed prompted.

''The way you looked at Sophie,'' Lara said in a rush. ''If I hadn't seen that, I might have even given in.''

''And how did I look at Sophie?''

''Like you wanted to devour her whole.'' Lara looked up at him with a wistful expression. ''I knew then that I was right for not giving in, that we would both be sorry. It made me realize that we shouldn't settle for second best ever again. We did once, and look what happened.''

Reed's troubled gaze met his ex-wife's. ''What are you saying?''

''That I want a man to look at me that way. That whatever it was that you and Sophie had hasn't gone away. There's still a spark there. Maybe it's something that can be fanned into a bigger flame. Maybe not. But you won't know until you pursue it.''

''She despises me.''

''So it won't be easy. You haven't become one of the best attorneys in southern Arkansas by taking the easy route.'' She clutched his arm and gave it a shake. ''I'm saying you've got to try, Reed. You owe it to yourself to try, or you'll always wonder if you let what might have been the best thing that ever happened to you slip away, not once but twice.''

Reed was never more glad to have had this woman be a part of his life. She'd been as wounded as he when they'd married, and pregnant, to boot. He hadn't known who the father was—Rowland and Phil had said it was a date rape—and hadn't cared. He'd been too wrapped up in his own guilt and misery to offer anything more than token resistance to his dad's urgings that he marry her to ''forget that little Delaney tramp'' and to ''help a good girl out of a terrible situation.'' He'd liked Lara, couldn't imagine the shame she must be feeling, so he'd allowed himself to be pushed into marriage. They'd both allowed it.

But three weeks after the wedding, Lara had lost the baby, and there had been no reason to stay married. They'd both grieved in their own way for their losses, but in the end it had been easier to drift into a true marital relationship than to dissolve the union.

For all that they'd tried, the marriage hadn't worked. Not even Belle's arrival could do anything more than postpone the inevitable. Somewhere along the way Reed had called Sophie's name at the point of his climax, and that had been the beginning of the end. The sad thing had been that it hadn't even upset Lara unduly. When she'd asked him, he'd told her the whole story about his brief ill-fated affair with Sophie Delaney. Lara had never reciprocated. To this day he had no idea which of his acquaintances had forced himself on his ex-wife.

Eventually Lara had insisted on ending their marriage, and Reed had agreed, because he knew she deserved better than he was able to give her. The good part was that they'd managed to salvage an important part of their relationship. They'd remained good friends, which was what they'd been all along.

The first thing Sophie did when she got home was put in a call to her cousin. Justine answered on the third ring, clearly pleased to hear from Sophie again so soon.

"So how is life in the boondocks?"

"Peaceful. We're all working like dogs, but the place is really coming around," Sophie said.

"That's good."

"How are you feeling?" Sophie asked.

"Well, the good news is that I'm not so sick now, but the bad news is that I'm starting to lose my figure." Justine laughed. "Maybe Pete was right after all. Maybe this wasn't such a good idea."

"You don't mean that."

"No," Justine said on a soft expulsion of air, "I don't."

"I saw your mother at the Woodcutters' Festival today. Have you talked to her lately?"

"No."

No explanation, just a flat denial. "Then you may not know. She has cancer, and evidently, it's pretty far advanced." No sound came over the line. Sophie couldn't even hear her cousin breathing. "You should give her a call, Justine. Better yet, you should come home and see her." When there was still no answer, Sophie prompted. "Justine?"

"I'm still here. But I can't come back. I can't."

"Look, I have no idea what happened between the two of you, but she's dying, Justine. You need to make your peace before she goes. If you don't you may never forgive yourself."

"It's her I can never forgive."

Sophie knew she wasn't about to break down the hard wall of resentment surrounding her cousin's heart. She also knew that if it wasn't destroyed, it would destroy Justine. But now wasn't the time to press. Justine had a good heart. News of her mother's illness was bound to diminish the ill feelings between them. Hopefully, she would come to her senses before it was too late. "If you won't come, at least call her."

"Maybe."

"She's your mother, Justine. She loves you."

"I don't want to hear it!" Justine said in a sharp voice.

"Maybe not, but just remember that never is a long time."

Desperate for a diversion, troubled by Lara's assessment of the situation with Sophie, Reed called Elissa and arranged to spend the rest of the day with her in Little Rock. They went to the art museum and to a movie, but not even the mentally taxing psychological thriller could hold his attention for more than a few minutes. In spite of everything, his thoughts kept returning to his conversation with his ex-wife. If he were honest with himself, and he prided himself on his honesty, he would admit that she was right. He still felt something for Sophie Carlisle, even if it was nothing more than desire.

Okay. So you still have a yen for her. No big deal.

But as much as he tried to convince himself that his feelings were nothing but desire, an inner voice kept whispering that it was more than that and that he owed it to himself to explore those feelings or he'd be sorry for the rest of his life. Reed didn't want that. God knew he had enough to be sorry for.

Sensing his distraction, Elissa declined coffee and dessert, and he drove her home straight after the movie, apologizing for his lack of interest, and laying blame on the custody suit coming up on Monday.

He'd barely made it home and traded his slacks and shirt for some shorts when there came a peremptory knock at the guest house door. Before Reed could bid the visitor to come in, the door was pushed open, and his father strolled in. Rowland's still-handsome face wore a friendly smile; the look in his eyes was anything but.

"Come on in, Dad," Reed said, indicating a chair with an expansive gesture.

Insensitive to or ignoring the sarcasm that Reed hadn't bothered to mask, Rowland plopped into a wing chair and crossed one expensively clad leg over the other. Reed grasped a dining table chair and straddled it, folding his arms across the back. "What's up?"

"I thought I should come and talk to you about Sophie Delaney."

Reed struggled to hide his surprise and his anger. "What about her?" he asked with as much nonchalance as he could muster.

"I saw you talking to her at the festival this morning. It appeared to me that you were flirting with her."

Evidently, he wasn't very good at hiding his feelings, Reed thought with dismay. Both Lara and his dad had recognized his interest in Sophie.

"I wouldn't consider it flirting," he said, refusing to offer any explanation for his actions. What had transpired between he and Sophie was no one's business but theirs.

"I know you don't think it's any of my business," Rowland said, echoing Reed's thoughts.

"It isn't."

"I just wanted to remind you that people in this town have long memories."

"Get real, Dad. No one in town knows I dated Sophie Delaney except you, me, Lara and Phil Grayson, and Phil's dead."

"It isn't the past that worries me as much as the future."

Reed laughed, but the sound held no mirth. "I spoke to her at a festival. I hardly think anyone would make much of that, not even in Lewiston. Besides, Sophie isn't the poor girl from the wrong side of the tracks anymore. She's a successful psychologist."

"She can still…hurt you."

"I'm not still carrying a torch for her, Dad," Reed said, but even as he spoke the words, he knew they weren't completely true.

A skeptical expression filled Rowland's eyes. "I hope not. Don't get involved with her, son."

Reed felt his hackles rise. He was finished with Rowland's attempts to control his life. "That sounds like a warning."

"No. Just a word of advice," Rowland said.

"I'm thirty-six years old. My personal life is none of your business, and I don't need your advice. And while we're on the subject, you can forget my getting any more involved with Elissa Markham. She's a nice woman, but she bores me senseless."

Rowland's lips thinned, all pretense of subtlety

gone. He glared at Reed. "Obviously, there's no talking to you."

"Obviously." Reed stood and headed for the door. "I'll see you out."

Rowland pushed himself to his feet, conceding the battle but never the war. He paused and pinned Reed with what came close to passing as a concerned expression. "Your glands got you into trouble with that little hussy once. I just don't want you to do anything foolish."

"You know, Dad, I've spent my life being the perfect, dutiful son, and it's a role that's wearing a little thin. The older I get the more I understand why Wes is determined to live his life the way he wants and the consequences be damned."

"Wes Grayson is, and always was, a disappointment to the Grayson name."

"Yeah, well," Reed said in a cutting tone, "you'd never prove it by his bank balance. Good night, Dad."

For once in his life, Rowland had the grace to keep quiet. Turning on his heel, he marched down the steps and along the flagstone path that led to the main house. Reed closed the door, knowing he'd infuriated his father, and curiously pleased by the fact.

Chapter Seven

Sophie spent a miserable Saturday afternoon and a sleepless night recalling every nuance of her meeting with Reed at the festival the day before. Longing to be too tired to even think about Reed, she spent most of Sunday hanging wallpaper with Cassidy while Donovan and Jett started putting up the heavy plastic on the framework of the first greenhouse.

They called it a day at five, and Jett approached an exhausted Sophie about taking Cassidy to the movies. Recalling Donovan's words, which she decided were pretty wise for a single man, Sophie gave in. She instructed them to be home by midnight, which, even allowing driving time home from the bigger city, should give them time to watch the movie and grab a late meal.

Jett left to get cleaned up; Cassidy did the same, then flipped through the TV channels while she waited for him to return. "Why don't you and Uncle Donovan get a shower and grab a sandwich in town?"

"Oh, Cass, I think I'm too tired," Sophie said, raking a weary hand through her hair.

"It has been a long day. Where is Uncle Donovan, anyway?"

"He drove over to talk to Isabelle Duncan about the work at the high school she mentioned. He doesn't want to let her down."

"She's strange," Cassidy said. "She kept staring and staring at me. She said I reminded her of someone, but she couldn't place who."

"She's old, Cass, and eccentric."

"No kidding. But it was kinda creepy with those little black eyes of hers, like she was trying to see into my soul or something."

"She's really very nice, and she has a big heart."

"That's what Belle said. Strange but nice." A knock sounded at the door. Cassidy let Jett in and came back to press a kiss to Sophie's cheek. "If you won't go out to eat, I think you should take a hot bath and have an early night."

"Good idea, Mom," Sophie said with a smile. She waved at Jett, who was waiting in the doorway. "Drive carefully."

"I will, Mrs. Carlisle. Good night."

Sophie listened as their footfalls clattered down the steps. She heard the slamming of the doors and the growl of Jett's truck engine as he peeled out of the driveway.

Kids! Though she'd never admit it to Cassidy, Sophie was glad there was no steady boy in her daughter's life. She knew all too well about the temptations that went hand in hand with young love. Thank goodness they would only be in Lewiston another week, not enough time for Jett and Cassidy to get too close. Or was there? It had only taken three dates for Reed to breach her defenses.

Stop it, Sophie! Cassidy isn't you, and Jett Robbins isn't Reed Hardisty. No, but as Donovan had pointed out, he was a lot like him at that age, and Donovan had had a way with girls even back then. What was it about a bad boy that made girls sit up and take notice? Was it the challenge in their eyes? The belief down deep in every young girl's heart that she could be the one to make him walk the straight and narrow? She shook her head. Cassidy would be fine. She was a lot more secure at sixteen than Sophie had been. She didn't need a sexual relationship with a bad boy to prove that she was wanted and loved the way Sophie had. And Reed hadn't been a bad boy.

What was it about him that had tugged so at Sophie's heart? His money? No. Getting a date with a guy from his social strata was quite a coup, but money in and of itself had never held much appeal. Maybe it had been Reed's vulnerability, his admission that his relationship with his dad wasn't the best, something Sophie could relate to. But money, no.

She didn't deny that it had been nice when Jake started making good money, and it was even nicer to know that he'd left her and Cassidy well provided for in his death, but she'd much rather have had him. There was little comfort in cold, hard cash. Sophie sighed. She missed him. Missed their easy camaraderie, their fighting. The lovemaking.

Without warning an image flashed through her mind: Reed cradling her cheek at the festival the day before, the way her blood raced when he touched her…the way he made her feel when he kissed her. *Whoa, Sophie! That was a long time ago.* Of course it was. But if the way he looked at her and the way she responded to his touch was any indication, his technique had improved through the years.

She knew that raking over the coals of their past was an exercise in futility, still, she couldn't help wondering if he ever thought about her and Cassidy. What had gone through his mind when he'd seen Cassidy at the Dairy Delight the night they first arrived? Donovan hadn't mentioned anything about Reed's reaction—or that he'd even had a reaction, coming face-to-face with his daughter, but surely it had affected him in some way. Maybe that's why he was seeking her out, Sophie thought. Maybe he was having regrets.

And maybe you're imagining things. Maybe her run-ins with him were nothing but coincidence. No, she thought. Donovan was convinced he'd come to the house to see her, and she knew Reed had deliberately struck up a conversation with her at the festival. It would have been easy to ignore her, to just walk by and pretend he hadn't seen her, but he hadn't, and the *why* was about to drive Sophie crazy.

Don't think about him. She sighed a sigh of frustration and irritation. She had no business thinking any tender thoughts about Reed Hardisty, no matter how good-looking he might be or how she reacted to him. She pushed herself to her feet. What she needed was what Cassidy had suggested a hot shower and an early night.

Sophie stood beneath the spray until the water ran cold, then toweled herself dry and put on a pair of white shorts and a lime-green scoop-necked top. The shower hadn't helped. All it did was make her more aware of her body and how long it had been since it had been touched by anyone's hands but hers. Telling herself her feelings were normal and healthy didn't make them any less acceptable.

She'd tried to think about Jake, but every time she closed her eyes, it was Reed's face she saw, Reed's voice she heard. And no wonder. She had never truly dealt with their past. Oh, she'd been through the anger, she'd pointed the finger of blame at him, she'd tried to block out what had happened by never talking about it, by staying away from Lewiston at all costs and never confessing the truth of Cassidy's paternity to her, as Jake had begged her to do. She sighed.

Her marriage to Jake had been as close to heaven on earth as any person was likely to find. They'd been compatible in many ways, direct opposites in others, but the thing that had made their marriage so strong was Jake's complete honesty and his willingness to see both sides of an issue, something he'd taught her through the years. Maybe what she should do, and hadn't, was try to put herself in Reed's place.

Whatever motivated him, Sophie knew it was past time to stop feeding her own bitterness. It was time to stop placing blame and try to come to terms with the past. Maybe if she understood where Reed had been coming from, she'd be better able to appreciate his decision.

She'd tried to imagine how he felt when her father told him and his dad that she was expecting his baby. Shocked? Angry? He'd already confessed to guilt for taking her virginity. Did that guilt extend to his fathering a child he didn't want? Had any part of him—

even a small part—wanted to be involved in their child's life and in hers? Just how much of his decision had been influenced by his father? What must it be like to tangle with a man like Rowland Hardisty?

The more she thought about it, the more certain she grew that Reed's father's wishes had influenced his decision. Letting his dad's feelings sway his ultimate judgment didn't make what Reed had done right, but neither did it make him a terrible person. Mightier men than Reed had bowed to the wills of men like Rowland Hardisty. And Reed had been young. They'd both been so young....

Sophie felt a tear trickle down her cheek. She brushed it away, determined not to let emotions rule her judgment, determined to reach some sort of understanding and find the closure she needed after so many years. Acting on pure impulse, driven by a force she didn't even try to understand, she grabbed the keys to Donovan's Explorer and drove to the lover's lane where she'd lost her innocence to Reed.

By the time she got there, she realized just how ridiculous the action was. Uncertain now of what she hoped to gain, but not yet ready to go back to the house, she put the car in park, opened the door and got out. Thankfully, there wasn't much chance of interrupting anyone's amorous ventures; there was too much daylight left for anyone to be parking just yet.

She drew in a deep breath of the country-fresh air. South Arkansas was being blessed with unusually cool weather for mid June. A soft breeze rustled the leaves of the massive black gum tree where Reed had parked the Firebird he'd gotten for his eighteenth birthday. Memories sapped her strength, and she placed her palms against the rough bark of the tree.

Like someone practicing the art of telekinesis, it seemed she drew memories from the tree. Her mind spun back…back. Sophie moaned at the onslaught of recollections. There had been heat. The hottest day of the summer. Michael Jackson on the radio. She covered her ears to block out the memory of her sobbing, and turned her back to the tree. It didn't help. She felt the emptiness that had swept down on her when Reed had gotten out of the car and left her crying in the back seat, her clothes awry, knowing already that she'd given herself to him for nothing. He would never be hers.

Now, as then, tears slipped down her cheeks, and she made no attempt to stop them. She hadn't cried over the past for a long time. Years, in fact. Maybe she needed the tears to wash away the last of the bitterness. Was there anything so painful as youth? Were there any adult challenges that matched the difficulty of simply growing up? But grown up she had, and so had Reed.

Reed. Standing in the shade of the gum tree with the wind whipping tendrils of still-damp hair around her face, Sophie let her mind drift back to her meeting with him at the festival. As angry as it made her to admit it, she'd responded to him in the same way she had the night he'd shown up on the pretext of telling Donovan about Blake Meriweather. Furious. Flustered. And very aware of him as a man, despite the way he'd treated her in the past.

Her reaction to him was most definitely physical. How could it be anything else? For all that she'd been intimate enough with him to bear his child, Reed Hardisty was a stranger to her. The few heart-to-heart conversations they'd had were hardly enough to give her any deep insight to his character. A seventeen-year absence certainly didn't help. As much as it galled her to admit that she was as susceptible to normal human weaknesses as the next person, she admitted that what she felt for Reed was desire, plain and simple. The realization did not please her, but there was no sense in denying it. The important question was, *why* did he affect her so?

It was something patients had asked her countless times before. Why do I still love him when he treats me so badly? How can I feel anything for him after what he's done? She always spouted textbook answers—fear of being alone, low self-worth, codependency. She didn't think any of those answers applied to her own situation.

If she took a step back, forgot it was herself and Reed in question and examined the situation with professional detachment, she would have to say that there was a part of her who still remembered the good of their time together: the way he'd opened up to her, the way he made her feel more important than she knew she was. And she knew that a part of her still wanted to believe that he was all the things she'd hoped and dreamed he was, even though his actions had proved otherwise. As much as she experienced the very real and often ugly side of life through her patients, part of her still believed in fairy tales and white knights and happy endings. She could thank Jake for that.

The sound of an approaching car halted her memories. Darn! She looked around and noticed that the long shadows of late afternoon were dissolving into dusk. She'd stayed too long and would have to skedaddle if she didn't want to intrude on someone's passionate encounter.

The car that pulled into view was a Lexus the same model and color as Reed's. Cars in that price range would be rare in a town the size of Lewiston, but she had a hard time picturing the older, sophisticated Reed making out at a lover's lane. Still, her heart began to pound.

She started for her own vehicle and was within three yards of it when the sound of a voice calling her name halted her. It *was* Reed. She turned, willing her features to impassivity, certain the sound of her beating heart could be heard over the soft rustling of the leaves and the mournful cry of a dove.

Like her, he looked as if he'd showered and thrown on the first clothes he found: a pair of running shorts and a Razorback sweatshirt with the arms cut out that should have been thrown away years ago. Though she kept her eyes fixed on his face, Sophie was aware that his legs were well shaped and well muscled and that the hair covering that tanned, taut flesh was dusted with the same gold as his eyelashes.

"What are you doing here?" he asked, coming to a stop near her, but not so close he was invading her space.

What was that she heard in his voice? A question? Resentment? Surprise? She raised her chin. "I might ask you the same thing."

He regarded her thoughtfully for several seconds then said, "Honestly?"

"Yes," she said, her voice tinged with irony. "Why don't you try honesty for a change?"

Reed recovered from the sharpness of the barb in

a heartbeat. "Okay. Honestly, I've been thinking about you ever since I saw you yesterday."

Sophie's heart seemed to stop, then it recovered and began to beat out a slow, fearful rhythm. Was the world she'd built so carefully about to fall in around her? She wrapped her arms around her middle. "R-Really?"

"Yeah." Reed paused, as if he were searching for the right thing to say. "Ever since I saw you and your daughter at the festival, I've been thinking about a lot of things," he said, at last. "The past. Us." He shook his head, blew out a harsh breath and planted his hands on his hips. "I don't know why I drove up here. I just seemed...pulled toward the place."

It wasn't the answer she'd expected to hear.

"What about you?"

"What?" she asked, looking up at him, confused by the relevance of the question to what he'd just said.

"You came for the same reason, didn't you?" he asked with soft insistence. "Because you've been thinking about me, about...us. Together. Here."

She averted her eyes, afraid he'd see the truth in hers. She'd never been very good at lying. "No."

"Liar." Reed reached out and took her chin, forcing her to face him...and the past. His thumb brushed over her bottom lip, skimming its fullness and stealing what little breath she had left.

"Don't," she managed to say, but the words held more pleading than irritation.

"Why?" he asked. "Are you afraid to have me touch you?"

"No."

"Yes, you are. Admit it, Sophie," he said, sliding

his hand around to the base of her skull and tangling it in her damp hair. "You've been thinking about me, too."

Sophie felt her will melting beneath the heat of his gaze and the soft persuasion in his voice. "No!"

"Yes. You've been thinking about the two of us in the back seat of my car."

Her breath was coming fast and shallow, as if she were engaged in the very act he accused her of thinking about. And the memories...dear sweet heaven, the memories were buzzing around her head, spinning through her mind, tumbling over each other for supremacy. His hands. His mouth. On hers. Touching her everywhere, and everywhere his mouth or his hands touched, fanning the heat of their desire.

She stepped back, making him release her. "Stop it!" she said in desperation, uncertain if she meant to silence him or her own renegade thoughts.

"You're thinking about how we were so hot for each other we didn't even get our clothes off. Remember? You haven't forgotten what we had, and you still want me."

Why was he doing this? she wondered wildly. Of course she wanted him, but she couldn't let him know it. Wouldn't. What did he hope to gain—another conquest? And where was her backbone? She hadn't come this far to have every bit of self-worth she'd struggled so hard to gain be blown away by a few seductive memories and a gorgeous man with a silver tongue.

With supreme effort, she shored up her determination. "Don't flatter yourself, Reed," she said with commendable disdain. "You weren't that good."

Pivoting on her heel, she started toward the car.

She'd taken no more than three steps when her foot came down wrong in a slight depression. The pain that shot through her ankle was as sharp as her cry of agony. She hit the ground so hard she felt jolted to the bone.

Reed was beside her in an instant, reaching down and helping her to her feet. "Are you okay?"

"What do you care?" she snapped, her anger and the pain in her ankle flooding her eyes with tears. She tried and failed to break free and found she couldn't put her full weight on her ankle. "You never cared before."

He looked as if she'd slapped him. Unless it was a trick of the dying light, his face suffused with color. "You're hurting."

"When did that ever matter to you? Why don't you just leave me alone, Reed?" she cried. "It wasn't too hard for you to do before." She jerked free and took a step toward the Explorer, almost falling again when her ankle refused to take her weight.

She heard him curse as he scooped her up into his arms. Before Sophie could do anything more than open her mouth to protest, his mouth swooped down to cover hers. The kiss was everything she remembered. No, it was more. He didn't fool around with a rough, hard kiss of punishment. Punishment wasn't what he was after. He did what he did best. Persuade.

Sophie's hands were pressed against his chest, as if she hoped to keep him from getting too close, yet knowing that it was too late for such flimsy precautions. His chest was firm and his heart pounded out a heavy, savage rhythm beneath her palm. She remembered that heartbeat, had once listened to it race as her own slowed to normal. She groaned at the image in her mind and, despite the warning ringing in her soul, her arms crept around his neck. She thought he was walking, was certain of it when he set her down, her back against the side of the Explorer. She gave a small cry of denial.

"Shh."

She felt his lips on hers, as gentle as the brush of a fairy wing, and opened her eyes in wonder. She closed them again at the naked longing she saw in his. It was too much. He was too much. She couldn't...

He kissed her again and, at the same time, lowered his body against hers, flattening her breasts with his chest and pressing one hard thigh between hers. She arched her hips against him involuntarily, a simple action that betrayed her need.

Taking the gesture for capitulation, Reed's hands moved to her hips, jerking her against him. His tongue plunged into her mouth, hard and hot, letting her know without a doubt what was on his mind and sending a jolt of desire straight to the center of her womanhood. She whimpered in dismay, knowing she was playing the fool, knowing she was opening herself to more heartache, furious with herself because she couldn't find the resolve within herself to stop him.

As if he sensed her distress, his mouth gentled, and his movements slowed. The plundering of her mouth mutated into the slow, provocative mimicry of sex. She felt every thrust, every seductive stroke of his tongue deep inside her. Felt the moisture and the heat gathering in delicious anticipation.

He wanted it, too. The hardness of his body moving against her told her that. The idea that she had this effect on him was heady, intoxicating. She should stop him. And would. Soon. He started to draw back, sensing, as she did, that they were about to cross some invisible line, knowing, too, that it wasn't the smart thing to do.

With a little cry of protest Sophie wound her arms around him more tightly, pressed harder—wanting, searching, needing…and hating herself for it. The craving was like a fire, licking hotly through her body, along her veins, igniting nerve endings, singeing, sizzling… She was hot, feverish. Burning. Uncaring that destruction would come in the aftermath of the conflagration.

And then it was too late to do anything more than feel. She balanced on the edge of eternity. Was sure that her heart and her breathing stopped. Felt nothing but the throbbing of release as she went into complete meltdown.

Reality returned slowly—the hardness of the sports utility vehicle behind her back, the whisper of the breeze in the trees, the scent of some green-smelling soap and a masculine cologne. Reed holding her tightly. Her face pressed against his shoulder. The feel of his thigh pressed intimately against her.

Sanity wormed its way into her consciousness, quickly followed by shame. Surely she hadn't just done what she thought she had. Knew she had. Embarrassment overrode her ability to think. Emotion overcame the need to save face. With a cry of mortification, with the last faint pulsing of her release throbbing through her, Sophie released her hold on Reed's neck and insinuated her hands between them.

"Let go of me."

Reed's only concession to her demand was to move his hands from her bottom to her shoulders. "Sophie…"

The tenderness in his voice unraveled the last thread of her composure. Tears welled up in her eyes and spilled over the fragile dam of her eyelashes. "Don't," she choked, pushing harder and turning her face away from him.

"Don't beat yourself up over this. It's no big deal."

That sent her gaze flying to his. "No big deal? I let you…let you…"

"Sophie." His voice was low, calm, reassuring. "Nothing happened."

"How can you say that?" she cried, resorting to anger in order to hide her humiliation.

With a smile he pushed himself away from her and held his arms out. "Look. Nothing happened. We're fully clothed. I gave you a moment's pleasure." His grin grew lopsided; his voice was filled with irony as he said, "I wish I could say the same for myself."

Sophie felt her face grow hot with the heat of a blush, but just knowing that he'd been as aroused as she didn't assuage her guilt or her embarrassment. She swiped at her wet eyes, turned and reached for the Explorer's door.

He put his hand out to keep her from opening the car's door. "Sophie, please."

She glared over her shoulder at him. "Why are you doing this?" she asked, pinning him with her tear-drenched eyes.

"Doing what?" he asked with a frown.

"Following me."

"I'm not following you."

"The festival—"

"So we both happened to be at the festival. Along with several hundred other people," he interrupted, his own irritation on the rise. "Trust me. I didn't follow you there. And how was I supposed to know you'd turn up here? Considering how you feel about me, it's the last place I'd have expected you to be. But here we are."

Yes, here they were.

"You're upset because I kissed you and—"

"It wasn't just a kiss—"

"—you got so hot—"

"—it was an *assault*."

"—and bothered that I brought you to a climax."

His statement elicited a stunned gasp and precluded any further argument. Before she could stop herself, before she even realized what she was about to do, she swung her hand toward his cheek with all her might.

Reed's reflexes were quick enough to stop the blow just inches from its target. His fingers bit into the flesh of her wrist. When she reached up to pry them loose, he captured her other hand and pinned both of them to the car door just above her head.

His face was mere inches from hers. His brown eyes glittered with displeasure. "Do you think I *like* this?" he said, his voice a low, angry rasp. "I've spent half my life trying to forget you, and the first time I set eyes on you in seventeen years I forget all the bad stuff. Worse than that," he continued, "the first time I get near you I can't remember anything but the way you taste, the way you felt in my arms, the way it felt to bury myself in you."

He paused and dragged in a deep breath of air, his

nostrils flaring in fury. "Do you think it makes me happy that you still have that effect on me?"

"You want to know something, Reed? I don't care!"

They stood there, glaring at each other, acutely aware that only inches separated bodies that were taut with awareness, each hating themselves for feeling anything for the other, both knowing that they had entered treacherous waters.

"Let me go," she said, the expression in her eyes warning him that she'd had enough.

Without another word he released her and stepped back so she could open the door. Her left leg refused her weight and her fanny plopped onto the car's seat.

"Someone should take a look at that ankle," he told her as she swung her legs in and started to pull the door shut. "My dad—"

"Can go straight to Hades," she said, and slammed the door in his face. She peeled out, leaving Reed standing in a cloud of dust. Her last image was of him looking after her, his legs spread apart and his hands planted on his hips.

The car took a curve and Sophie lost sight of him. She'd lied about not caring about his feelings. She'd lied because she was terrified of facing the truth. She cared. Far more than the common sense she prided herself on having told her she ought to.

It was almost full dark by the time Sophie got back to Donovan's place. His truck was sitting in front of the house when she pulled into the driveway, and the light was on in the kitchen. Darn! she thought. Why couldn't she have had a few minutes to get herself together before having to face anyone? She wondered if her brother would be able to tell what had happened between her and Reed by the look on her face.

He'd have to be psychic.

Well, sometimes it seemed he was. She sighed, got out of the vehicle and slammed the door, clinging to the fender and hood as she made her way toward the porch steps. Every step was pure agony. As she grabbed the doorjamb, the door opened, and she faced her brother, whose handsome face wore a frown.

"Where the hell have you been?"

"When did I have to start checking in with you?" Sophie snipped.

"Ah," he said, a knowing expression in his eyes, "been up to something you shouldn't have, have you?"

"I don't know what you're talking about," she said, releasing her hold on the door frame and hobbling toward the table.

"Sure you do, but I don't. Not really." He reached out and took her arm, and she leaned on him heavily. "Just guessing. Seems like we always get defensive when we've been doing something we shouldn't." He pulled out a chair for her. "What happened?"

"I turned my ankle. It's sprained, I think."

"Where were you?"

"Wolf Creek Plateau."

Donovan's eyebrows lifted in surprise. "Not much fun by yourself," he said. "You *were* alone?"

The gaze that met his was steady, defiant. "I went alone," she said, refusing to volunteer anything more.

"Had company, did you? Reed, I assume." When Sophie didn't answer, he said, "Did you arrange to meet him there at the festival?"

Her eyes flashed. "I most certainly did not."

Donovan held his palms out, as if to keep her anger back. "I believe you."

"Good. Because I don't want to talk about it."

"So I gather." He dragged a chair around and sat down facing her. "Swing that leg up here, and let me take a look."

He probed and poked and grunted in a purely male way that told her nothing and finally pronounced that the ankle was indeed sprained. "It's already swelling," he announced, "and there's some bruising. You might want to get a doctor to look at it, just to be sure."

"Not Rowland Hardisty."

"There's another doctor in town," Donovan reminded her.

"Just put an elastic bandage around it," she told him, resting her weary head in her hand. "It's a long way from my heart."

Donovan chuckled and set about wrapping her ankle. He gave her a couple of tablets for the pain, helped her to her feet and told her to go to bed.

"Try to get some sleep," he said. "Tomorrow we're going to have a nice long talk."

"About what?" she asked.

Donovan's smile held not a trace of humor. "Those whisker burns on your face, for starts."

Chapter Eight

Sophie could tell from the look on Donovan's face the next morning that he meant business. He helped her to a chair, propped her foot on another, poured her a mug of coffee and sat down across from her, a patient, waiting expression on his face. Sophie knew she could make her life a lot easier by cooperating with him.

"Okay, okay!" she said. "I drove out to the plateau. I don't know why. I hadn't been there long when Reed showed up...."

The sound of her mother and uncle talking awakened Cassidy. Usually, her uncle Donovan went outside to work on whatever project he was tackling, and her mother went about her business as quiet as a proverbial mouse.

Cassidy stretched and thought about Jett. They'd

done some pretty heavy kissing the night before and more petting than she knew she should have, considering that she hadn't known him all that long. She knew she couldn't let things go too far. She knew the score. She didn't plan to let an unplanned pregnancy mess up her life, and she didn't want Jett to think she was a tease. There was no alternative but to cool things down, which shouldn't be too hard, since she'd be going back to Baton Rouge soon.

Cassidy rolled to her side, pushing thoughts of Jett Robbins aside and trying to force herself to get up and face the day. Without meaning to, she picked up on the conversation in the kitchen again. Though their voices were muted, almost as if they were trying not to wake her up, her mother sounded angry. No, not angry exactly, but on the defensive. There wasn't much feedback from her uncle. Maybe she should go put an end to whatever it was they were arguing about.

Cassidy was out of bed and had her hand on the doorknob when it occurred to her that their conversation might be private. She hesitated, uncertain whether or not she should interrupt. Then she heard her mother's voice again. Now it sounded as if she might be crying. Cassidy put her ear to the door.

"I let him kiss me, Donovan," Cassidy heard her mother say. "But then, you'd already figured that out, hadn't you?"

Cassidy's mouth fell open. Her mother had let some man kiss her? Who?

"Hey, it happens," Donovan said. "I've known ever since we got here that he's been on your mind. How could he not be?"

"Yeah, well, evidently, I've been on his, too. He

said he'd spent half his life trying to forget me. What do you think he meant by that?''

''That he hasn't, obviously.''

Who was the ''he'' they were talking about? Cassidy wondered, a frown puckering her smooth forehead, her heart hammering. Who had tried and failed to forget her mom? Some high school sweetheart? And if she'd kissed him, her mom must still have feelings for him, too.

''And how was it?'' she heard her uncle say.

''What?'' her mother asked.

''The kiss.''

Cassidy heard her mother groan. ''Kisses,'' she clarified. ''And don't ask. I don't want to think about it. Or him.''

There were a few seconds of silence, and then her mom spoke again. ''When he said he'd seen me and Cassidy together, I was so afraid he was going to ask me about her, maybe want to start seeing her on a regular basis or something. I could see my whole world falling in around me. Darn you, Donovan! I should never have let you talk me into coming back.''

''You're a big girl,'' Cassidy heard him say in his usual no-nonsense tone. Her uncle was big on a person taking responsibility for his actions. ''You've known every time you brought her back there was a chance he'd confront you about her.''

Cassidy frowned. What man might confront her mother about her—and why?

''You should have listened to me and Jake, Sis. You should have told Cass the truth long ago.''

''I couldn't,'' Cassidy heard her mother say in a ragged, teary voice that tore at Cassidy's heart. She

knew that sound. Her mother was in pain, as much
pain as she'd suffered when her dad died.

"She loves you, Sophe. Nothing will ever change
that. Not even finding out that Reed Hardisty is her
real father."

Cassidy clamped her free hand over her mouth to
hold back a cry of shock and despair. She backed
away from the door as if there were something hei-
nous on the other side.

"You'd better find a place and a time to tell her,
before she finds out some other way," her uncle said.

Too late, Uncle Donovan. Too late. The backs of
Cassidy's legs hit the edge of the bed, and she sat
down hard. Her mind raced, the words she'd heard
echoing in her head while a voice inside her screamed
that it couldn't be true. No way. Jake Carlisle was her
father. Had always been. Weren't there pictures of the
two of them, taken the day she and her mom came
home from the hospital? And before that, there was
a snapshot of her dad with his head against her mom's
swollen belly, a big, sappy grin on his face. Reed
Hardisty couldn't be her real dad. He couldn't!

Cassidy wasn't even aware that tears had begun to
slip down her cheeks. If it was true, and there was
simply no way it could be—but *if*—then her mother
had done something unthinkable. She had tricked Jake
Carlisle into thinking another man's baby was his.
And if that was true, then her mother, who had
stressed the importance of telling the truth, had lied.
To everyone.

Cassidy clutched her aching head, her gaze glancing around the room, her thoughts a wild tangle of
indecision. What should she do? What should she
say? Should she go out and tell them what she'd over-

heard? No. Not right now. She needed to find out the truth, and evidently, if it was truth she wanted, her mom wasn't the person to talk to.

Fueled with disappointment and anger, Cassidy refused to listen to the voice inside her that whispered that her mother was upset, was *worried* about her finding out. Of course she was worried and upset, Cassidy thought bitterly. She didn't want Cassidy to know she'd been living a lie.

Jett arrived, and Donovan went outside to start the day's work. Sophie sat with her foot propped up, her thoughts—as painful as her ankle—ricocheting from her disastrous encounter with Reed the night before to Donovan's warning that she should tell Cassidy the truth about Reed.

Sophie knew he was right. She had to tell Cassidy before someone let it slip. *Like who? Reed?* It seemed impossible to think he would do that, but sometimes a person did crazy things for crazy reasons—like a perverted sense of doing the right thing when all he really wanted was to clear his conscience. Or gain retaliation for old wrongs. The problem was that from Sophie's perspective she was the one who'd been wronged, not Reed.

Still, it was something to consider. Even though Reed had rejected her and Cassidy, some egotistical part of him might have felt wronged because she'd moved and taken Cassidy away. Was he capable of revenge? Would he tell Cassidy the truth to get at her? And was the need to punish her behind his seduction of her the night before? She thought of his kisses and the willful way her body had reacted to him. If he'd set out to use submission or embarrass-

ment as a form of vengeance, he'd certainly suc-
ceeded.

Cassidy sauntered into the dining area, still in her
nightclothes, putting an end to Sophie's thoughts. Her
daughter looked tired, Sophie thought, and maybe as
if she'd been crying. "Hi."

"Hi," Cassidy said. She hardly looked at Sophie
but headed straight for the coffeepot to pour some of
the freshly brewed liquid into a mug. "How's the
ankle?"

"Much better," Sophie said. "There isn't much
bruising. I'll stay off it today and see how things go.
How about you? You look wiped out."

And Cassidy was avoiding looking at her, too,
which usually signaled guilt for something. Sophie's
fears about Cassidy succumbing to Jett's attentions
returned with a vengeance.

"I am, and I have a headache." Cassidy sat down
and, almost deliberately it seemed, raised her gaze to
her mother's. "Is it okay if I skip out on you this
morning and go swimming at Belle's?"

"Is it okay with Belle's mother?"

Cassidy dropped her eyelashes and stared at her
coffee cup. "Yeah. Jett and I ran into them at the
Dairy Delight last night, and they invited me then."

*Let her go. She isn't sneaking off to meet Jett. He's
here, working.* "It's fine with me, then," Sophie said,
unable to shake the idea that something was off-kilter.

"Thanks, Mom." Cassidy's gratitude was accompanied by a too-bright smile.

Sophie frowned. It was possible that Jett was putting pressure on Cassidy, and it was troubling her.
Maybe she just needed a day to herself to get her
mind straight. And then, maybe she was imagining

things. But Sophie knew her daughter pretty well. Something was definitely bothering her. She also knew that Cassidy was good at working things out for herself. All she needed was time, and she'd figure out the best way to handle her problem—whatever it was.

After gulping down a bowl of corn flakes, Cassidy showered, dressed and escaped the house, taking the Explorer, promising she'd be careful, saying she wasn't sure what time she'd be home. Which was true. By being unspecific about the time of her return, she'd gained several hours to contemplate what to do about the conversation she'd overheard.

She had to get to the truth. She could ask her uncle, but he'd just go tell her mom, and she wasn't ready to face her just yet. The urge to tell someone about her predicament was overwhelming, but who? Jett was working with her uncle, and the only other person she knew who might listen was Belle...Reed Hardisty's daughter.

A sudden thought made Cassidy gasp. If it was true, if Reed was her father, too, then she and Belle were sisters. The thought almost caused Cassidy to run a stop sign. The thought of having Belle as a sister was as sobering as it was pleasing. Cassidy had always wanted a sister. Is that why she and Belle had taken to each other so quickly? And how could she tell Belle what she'd overheard without causing her pain?

Pretend it's something else. A hypothetical situation. At least you can get some sort of feedback, even if it is from a twelve-year-old.

Desperately needing to talk to someone, Cassidy drove straight to the house Belle shared with her mother and rang the doorbell before she could change her mind. Lara Hardisty answered the door almost immediately.

"Hello, Cassidy," she said, surprised. "What brings you out so early?"

"Oh, I'm sorry!" Cassidy said in genuine distress. "Is it too early to see Belle a minute?"

Lara Hardisty stepped back with a smile, but there was a curious expression in her dark eyes. No doubt she was wondering why Cassidy was seeking out Belle. "No. She's awake. And it isn't that early at all. Go on up. You know where her room is."

"Thank you." Cassidy started for the stairs.

"Cassidy?"

"Ma'am?" Cassidy said, turning.

"Is everything okay?"

"Yes, ma'am," Cassidy fibbed. "Everything's fine. Just a little boy trouble." Which wasn't *exactly* another lie.

Belle's mother nodded, but the expression in her eyes didn't go away. Cassidy knocked on Belle's door, poking her head in at the same time. Belle was sprawled on her stomach, a banana in her hand, watching the cartoon channel. When she saw who was at her door, she beamed.

"Cassidy!" she cried, rolling off the bed and to her feet. "Come on in! What are you doing here?"

Cassidy couldn't help feeling pleased that her presence had such a positive effect on the younger girl. "I need to talk to you, Belle. I need to ask your opinion about something."

Belle sank back down onto the bed, flabbergasted. "*You* want *my* opinion about something? Wow!" She chomped off a big bite of banana. "What is it?" she asked around a mushy mouthful.

Cassidy sat down next to the girl who might be her sister. Belle's eyes were filled with curiosity, and Cassidy knew she had to choose her words carefully so Belle wouldn't know who she was talking about.

"What should you do if you overhear a conversation you weren't meant to overhear?"

"You were eavesdropping?" Belle squealed, her eyes wide with mortification. "Great-Aunt Isabelle says no good comes from eavesdropping."

Cassidy struggled to control her irritation. "I wasn't eavesdropping," she said. "Not really." Then she caught herself. "Good grief, Belle, I'm not even saying that it was me. We're just playing 'what if.'"

"Oh," Belle said with a slow nod. "I gotcha. So you—I mean, uh, *someone*—overheard something they weren't supposed to hear. Was it about them?"

"Yes," Cassidy said with a nod. "And what this person heard made their whole life a complete and total lie. Someone very close to…this person—actually several people—had lied to her about her relationship with someone she was very close to. She thought someone was one person, but in fact, someone else was really who she thought the other person was."

"I'm lost," Belle said, shaking her head.

"I know," Cassidy said. "It is confusing."

Belle was silent, and Cassidy stared, without really seeing them, at the hands knotted in her lap. She felt tears stinging beneath her eyelids. "It hurt m— uh, this person really bad, especially if what she heard is the truth, which she isn't sure of."

"Why doesn't this person just ask the people she heard talking if it's true or not?" Belle asked.

"Because she isn't sure she can face them right now. She's too upset. And I'm...I mean, *she's* pretty angry to think that she was lied to for so long."

"Oh." Belle pondered that for a moment. "Then she should ask the *other* person. The one she's close to, that the lie was about, who she thought was the real person...or whatever," Belle said with a baffled shrug.

Jake. "He's dead."

"Well, she's got to ask someone. Is there anyone else you—I mean, she—can ask?"

Yes! Cassidy wanted to cry. Reed Hardisty. Your father. "Well, there is someone who knows the truth, but if he does, then she's pretty angry at him, too, for not c-caring...." Cassidy sighed and blinked hard to hold back the tears. It was no use. Belle couldn't help her. No one could. She would have to figure it out for herself. Without saying anything else, she stood and headed for the door. "I've gotta go, Belle. Thanks for listening."

"Wait!" Belle cried, flinging herself off the bed and grabbing Cassidy's arm.

"What?" Cassidy hoped Belle wouldn't see the tears in her eyes, but knew she couldn't miss them.

"Sometimes people tell lies to keep from hurting someone. Like saying your mom looks pretty in a dress when you think it's awful, you know?"

Cassidy nodded.

"My dad's a lawyer. He says telling the truth is always the right thing to do, even if someone gets hurt. Otherwise, the lies get stacked on top of each other, and the truth is harder to find. If you'd have gone to him instead of coming to me, he'd have told you to ask the person who's most likely to tell the truth about what you overheard. And that's what I'm telling you.''

Then, to Cassidy's surprise, Belle put her arms around her and gave her a big hug. ''It'll be okay, Cassidy,'' she said with a smile of commiseration. ''Promise.''

Cassidy hugged Belle back and let herself out. As she went down the stairs, she thought that if she could have a sister, Belle would be a pretty neat one to have. She also knew that she had to find out the truth no matter how much it hurt. This wasn't the kind of thing you just forgot about. But who should she ask? Cassidy's emotions waffled between hurt and anger. Why hadn't they told her the truth? And who would?

My dad says…telling the truth is always the right thing to do…

Remembering what Belle had told her about her dad and considering that if what she'd overheard was true, Reed Hardisty was bound to know it, Cassidy figured she had no choice but to take her questions to him, no matter how hard it would be to face him.

Reed was sitting at his desk, a sheaf of papers in front of him, his thoughts centered on Sophie, as they had been for the better part of the night. Three things were certain: he still held the power to excite her sexually; Sophie still had the power to do the same to him; and Lara had been right—no one should settle for second best when it came to choosing a life's partner.

That thought stopped all others cold. Life's partner? Where had that come from? Was he seriously considering a life with Sophie Carlisle? How could he, when, despite the intimacy they'd shared, they were virtual strangers? Even though he'd proved that there was still some powerful force at work when they were together, that chemistry wasn't love. Never had been; never would be.

He thought about the fact that if they'd had a chance to explore their feelings seventeen years ago, those feelings might—if nurtured properly—have grown into something more, something deeper, but even that possibility didn't alter the fact that they'd both changed during the time they'd spent apart. Neither of them was the person they'd been as teenagers.

Physically Sophie was much the same. The years had only refined her features, giving her a quiet beauty that would serve her well through the next couple of decades. Emotionally she'd grown not only in experience and wisdom but in strength of character as well. The new Sophie had lost the insecurities that had rendered her shy to the point of painfulness, and if the sharpness of her tongue was any indication, she'd learned that she got better results from taking the offensive.

Lara was a spirited sort of woman, and Reed had grown to admire the trait. He admired Sophie for the way she'd taken a less-than-perfect life and turned it into one anyone could be proud of.

He wondered how her ankle was, and that thought led to the memory of pinning her to the car and of kissing her. Recalling the hunger of their kisses and the ease at which he'd brought her to the very peak of desire, an undeniable heat begin to rise inside him. He muttered a mild curse. Just the thought of her trembling on the brink of fulfillment excited him. He wanted to see her but knew the demands of his day precluded his leaving the office.

He could talk to her, though. She probably wouldn't like his calling any more than she would an impromptu visit, but he wasn't thinking about what she'd like or dislike, only of the urgent need to have some sort of contact with her. He asked information for Donovan's number, punched it in and waited for someone to answer.

"Hello."

Even the sound of her voice, low and a bit breathless, had the power to arouse feelings he knew he'd be smarter not to encourage. But Reed had played by the rules and taken the road of least resistance all his life, and this was one time he intended to be guided by nothing more than the moment's whim.

"Hi," he said. "It's Reed."

"Reed?"

"Yeah. I thought I'd call and check on you. I was worried about you...after what happened last night."

There was a long silence, and he knew she was thinking of their passionate kissing session. He could have sworn he heard her breathing soft and fast, the way he had when she'd broken away from him. He was afraid she would hang up on him, afraid she'd cuss him out for taking advantage of her. Afraid...

"So how is the ankle, anyway?" he asked, when it became apparent that she wasn't going to reply.

"Fine," she said in a bright voice, clearly relieved that he'd steered the conversation away from the personal. "The swelling seems to be going down. Donovan thinks I should stay off it today."

"That's smart," Reed said.

She gave a short laugh that betrayed her nervousness. "I'm not much good to him, though. I won't be able to get much done before I have to go home."

Reed felt a sharp pain in his heart. "When do you leave?"

"We were going to stay until the weekend, but I've been thinking about going back early since I can't do much with a sprained ankle."

"Don't do that." The words surprised him as much as they probably did Sophie.

"Wh-What?"

"Don't go back early." His voice grew stronger as he spoke. "Stay, Sophie. We need to talk about what happened last night."

"I don't want to talk about it," she told him, a distinct edge to her voice. "I don't even want to think about it."

"But you are, aren't you?" When she didn't reply, he prompted, "Aren't you, Sophie?"

"All right! Yes! But I don't want to."

"Me, either, but I'm thinking about it, too." He gave a short laugh. "In fact, I haven't been able to get much work done for thinking about it. We need to talk, Sophie. It isn't going to go away."

"There's nothing to talk about," she snapped. "And I'm going away." Then, as if she'd grown suddenly weary of fighting the memories, him, and maybe herself, her tone softened. "What happened shouldn't have. Especially not with you. I have no excuse except that it's been a long time since…since Jake died."

Ignoring the fact that there had been no one for her since her husband's death, he said, "Clarify why it especially shouldn't have happened with me. Why not me?"

He heard her suck in a sharp little breath. "You know why."

"I'm not sure I do. Is it because of what happened between us before?"

"Don't you think that's reason enough for me to steer clear of you?" she countered.

"Not necessarily. Like I've said before, we were kids. I didn't handle things as well as I should have, but I was scared."

"Of what?"

"I was scared of taking your virginity. I felt responsible somehow. And I was scared of how you made me feel. I wasn't sure I was ready for the kind of commitment I knew I owed you."

"Oh, you made that very clear," she said in a sardonic tone.

"By not calling, you mean?"

"Yes."

"Well, it backfired, because I still thought about you. I still think about you."

"Don't!"

"Why? I'm an adult now, Sophie. So are you. I'm not into denial anymore. I like to try to get to the bottom of things, to find out the truth, and I think we owe it to ourselves to get to the bottom of the feelings we still have for each other, whatever they may be."

"It's lust, Reed," she said in a hard, clipped voice. "Plain and simple lust."

"Is it?"

"Look," she said, the quaver in her voice betraying her emotion. "I don't want to be having this conversation. It's going nowhere. *We're* going nowhere. I'm hanging up now."

"Fine. But you're not getting off the hook that easily. I'll be in touch."

"Reed—"

He hung up before she could tell him not to call again, before she did. While he was still in control. He was shaking as badly as her voice had been. He propped his elbows on the desk, clasped his hands together and rested his forehead against them. He was committed now. Whatever happened he was committed to following through on his promise to explore their feelings for each other...wherever they might lead.

Reed's intercom buzzed, snapping his attention back to the moment. "Yes, Liz?"

"There's a young lady to see you, Mr. Hardisty."

Reed glanced at the clock. Lara was dropping Belle by at eleven so that he and his daughter could go to lunch. He frowned. Lara was usually a little early, but it was only ten-thirty. "Who is it?"

"Cassidy Carlisle."

He had no idea why Cassidy would come to see him, but she was Sophie's child, and anything that had to do with Sophie interested him. "Send her in."

A few seconds later Cassidy came through the door. Out of ingrained habit, Reed rose when she came into the room. He didn't know what he expected, but it wasn't what he saw. Cassidy's spine was straight, and her eyes blazed with determination and something akin to anger—indignation, maybe.

He frowned. "Come in, Cassidy. Have a seat."

"No, thank you," she said, striding across the width of the room to the window that looked out on an elm-lined street.

Put off by the emotion radiating from her, Reed

found that he was at a loss as to what to say, something unusual for him. "What can I do for you?" he asked when a few uncomfortable seconds ticked by.

She turned to look over her shoulder at him. "Belle says you're big on telling the truth."

Reed's confusion deepened. He had no idea why she'd come, and certainly no idea what she might have been talking to Belle about. "I try to make it a habit to be honest, yes," he told her.

She turned and crossed the room, coming to a stop in front of his desk and clutching the edge in a white-knuckled grip. "I need to ask you something, and I need you to be truthful."

"All right," he said, nodding.

Cassidy took a deep breath and plunged. "Are you my father?"

Reed regarded the young woman before him, hardly able to think for the numbing shock and the hundreds of thoughts whirling through his mind. "I beg your pardon?" he said, certain his shock must be stamped on his features. "Where did you get such an idea?"

"I overheard my uncle and my mother talking this morning. He said she should tell me the truth before I found out some other way, which means she's lied to me all these years about my dad—Jake—being my dad. So I'm asking you. Are you my biological father?"

While it was true that she looked a lot like Sophie, there was the matter of her hair, which was the color of his own…and of Belle's. And she had Belle's nose, too, he thought with more surprise. And that slight cleft in her chin…

Dear God, was it possible? Had Sophie been carrying his child when she packed up and left town? Had she tricked that other poor guy into thinking Cassidy was his baby? Why hadn't she come to him and told him? He'd have—

You'd have what, Hardisty? Offered to make an honest woman of her? You dumped her, remember?

He remembered all too well. It was something that had consumed his thoughts even during his marriage to Lara. If what Cassidy said was true, and it was entirely possible that it was, he knew Sophie well enough to know that telling him she was pregnant was the last thing she would have done....

Belle, who'd been dropped off by her mother, didn't see her dad's secretary at her desk. Liz had probably taken a bathroom break, so Belle decided she would just be real quiet and go on in. That way, if her dad was on the phone, she wouldn't bother him. She heard him talking to someone as she turned the knob and quietly pushed open the door a few inches. She was surprised to see Cassidy talking to her dad. Why was she here? And why did her dad look so pale and upset? Thankfully, Cassidy's back was to her, and her dad was too engrossed in their conversation to realize anyone was at the door.

She knew the discussion was private and was about to close the door when she heard her dad say, "Does your mother know you're here?"

"Never mind my mother!" Cassidy said angrily. "It's a simple yes or no question, Mr. Hardisty. Are you my father or not?"

Belle gripped the doorknob so hard her fingers hurt. She felt her eyes grow big and her mouth fall open in surprise. Her mother had told her the facts of life as preparation of her starting her period, and Belle knew that it took sex between two people to make a baby. But that would mean that her dad and Cassidy's mother... But sex was supposed to be saved for marriage. What was going on?

Belle saw her dad take a deep breath. "Truth, Cassidy?" he said. "The truth is that it's possible. I could be."

Belle gasped, and both her dad and Cassidy looked toward the door.

"Belle!" Cassidy said, her face a study in pain and sorrow.

Belle's dad raked his hand down his face and said a word she'd once got her mouth washed out for saying.

Without a word to either of them, Belle slammed the door shut and ran out of the office, as if she were being chased by a legion of demons. Great-Aunt Isabelle always said no good came from eavesdropping. She was right.

Reed watched as Cassidy turned and ran out of his office after Belle. Uncertain which crisis needed his attention first, he sank down into his burgundy leather chair. *Think, Hardisty, think!*

Damn! What a way for Cassidy—and him—to find out the truth...if it was the truth, and there was no reason for Donovan to encourage Sophie to tell Cassidy if it wasn't. Why hadn't he ever considered the possibility? Maybe, since he prided himself on his honesty, he should admit that the thought had, on occasion, crossed his mind, but he'd dismissed it because they'd been together only once.

And Belle—he groaned—what must she be thinking? As much as he wanted to go after Cassidy, as much as he wanted to confront Sophie, he knew his allegiance was to Belle. He picked up the phone and called Lara on her car phone. She probably hadn't even had time to get home.

Lara picked up on the second ring. Always a good listener, she didn't interrupt as he explained what had just transpired in his office.

"Do you know where they went?"

"No," Reed confessed, raking a hand through his hair. "They both went tearing out of here like a pack of mad dogs were after them."

"I'll drive around and look for Belle. She can't have gotten far on foot. I'll meet you at the house."

"I'm on my way."

"What about Cassidy?"

"I think she was going after Belle. Maybe we'll find them together." *And then I can call Sophie and we can all sit down and try to figure a way out of this unholy mess.*

Reed was aware of a slow burn whenever he thought of Sophie. If what Cassidy claimed was true and Sophie had kept the pregnancy a secret from him all these years... He swore. No wonder Cassidy was so angry. So was he.

Lara drove up and down the streets Belle might have taken to get home. She didn't see any signs of her daughter or Donovan's Explorer. Deciding that maybe somehow she had missed Belle and she was at the house, Lara drove home, calling Belle's name as she went from room to room. She didn't find her daughter anywhere in the house, but her answering machine was blinking monotonously.

Lara hit the play button and Sophie's voice filled the room. "Hi, Lara. This is Sophie Carlisle. It's getting near lunchtime and I was wondering if Cassidy is eating there, or coming home. She seemed a bit vague about how long she and Belle might swim." Lara heard Sophie sigh. "Anyway, if she's headed back this way, will you ask her to stop and pick up a loaf of bread? Thanks."

Lara erased the message and leaned against the kitchen cabinet, digesting what she'd just heard. Sophie didn't have a clue as to what was going on. Evidently, Cassidy's story was true. She'd overheard a conversation, bypassed any confrontation with her mom and headed straight for the other person she figured would know the truth.

When she and Reed married, they had exchanged the briefest information about their past relationships. Reed knew Lara was pregnant—indeed that was part of the reason for their marriage—but she'd never said by whom. She knew Reed had seduced Sophie and been plagued with such guilt he couldn't face her again. She honestly didn't think he'd known about Cassidy.

Lara's sigh echoed Sophie's. She would have to tell Reed about the phone message and let him deal with breaking the news to Sophie. This was not the sort of thing an ex-wife wanted to be in the middle of.

Chapter Nine

Cassidy was smart enough to get the Explorer before setting out after Belle. She caught up with the younger girl on a side street three blocks from the Hardisty law office. Cassidy rolled down the passenger side window and drove slowly alongside the girl who might be her sister. Belle spared Cassidy a brief glance then turned her gaze determinedly ahead.

"Get in the car, Belle."

"No, thank you."

Even though Cassidy had known Belle a short time, she recognized the set of her jaw and the fire in her eye for the anger it was. "Belle, please."

"I don't want to talk to you."

Cassidy's heart sank. Great. All she needed right now was another major problem in her life. "Don't be mad at me," she said. "I didn't do it."

Belle kept walking, and in spite of herself, Cassidy

felt tears spring into her eyes. The road blurred. She pulled to a halt at the curb, put the vehicle in park and folded her arms along the top of the steering wheel. The last thing she needed was to wreck her uncle's wheels.

To her surprise Belle stopped and turned around, curious, if nothing else. After a full minute of them just looking at each other, Belle began walking toward the car. She opened the door and got inside, rolling up the window, as if to seal them and their misery inside. She was crying, too. Cassidy raised the armrest, found some tissues in the storage console between the seats and handed Belle some.

"You think it's true, don't you?" Belle asked, wiping at her eyes.

"I don't know what to think," Cassidy said, dabbing at her own eyes.

They were silent for a moment, and then Belle said, "If it is true, it means that he and your mom had sex." She made a face at the thought.

An all-too vivid image of that very thing flashed through Cassidy's mind. She wasn't comfortable with the idea of her mom having sex with anyone. She was her mom, for heaven's sake! "I know."

"Do you think that's why my mom and dad got divorced?" Belle asked, fixing Cassidy with a troubled frown.

"No, of course not! Think, Belle. If it happened, it would have been before they got married. My mom would have been my age, and she'd never cheat with another woman's husband."

The idea of being sixteen, pregnant, poor and unmarried hit Cassidy like a freight train. Her anger at her mother lessened, but her dejection deepened. Now she understood her mom's near-paranoia about the subject of sex before marriage. Cassidy wondered what she'd do, if she found herself in the same predicament.

"So your mom told you someone else was your dad, right?" Belle asked.

Cassidy nodded. If she were in the same situation, would she do what her mother must have done and trick some other guy into thinking the baby was his? She didn't think she could do that, and it was hard to believe her mom would, either, but then, what guy would marry a girl knowing she was pregnant by someone else?

"This must be very hard for you," Belle said, surprising Cassidy once more—not only by being able to set aside her own shattered illusions and pain but by her ability to see things from a grounded viewpoint.

"You, too," Cassidy said.

"Yeah, but at least I know who my parents are. I mean, I know my dad is my dad." She chewed on her lower lip. "If it's true, I don't think he knew, do you?"

"He seemed surprised," Cassidy admitted.

"If it's true," Belle said, determined to get everything out, "then I guess that makes us sisters. Stepsisters."

"No. Half sisters," Cassidy corrected.

The corners of Belle's mouth turned down. "I always wanted a sister."

"Me, too," Cassidy said. *But not this way. Not by losing my dad.*

"What are you going to do? Talk to your mom?"

"I don't know," Cassidy said, feeling the sting of

more tears. "I'm not sure I can face her. She'll just try to explain things away, and that's not what I need right now. I need some time alone, to think. To grieve." She turned teary eyes to Belle's and pressed her palm against her heart. "I don't know how to explain it, but it hurts, Belle. It's like my dad—like Jake—has died all over again."

Belle nodded in sympathy. "I know a place you can go to be alone, if you want."

"Where?"

"My uncle Wes's house. He called my mom last week and said he was going to New Orleans for a few days. His house key is hanging right by our back door."

"I can't do that," Cassidy said. "It'd be like breaking and entering or something."

"No, it wouldn't. I'll be letting you in. Uncle Wes is cool. He won't care, as long as you don't mess with his paints and stuff."

Cassidy thought about it for a while, then, knowing that she desperately needed some time to gather her thoughts, nodded. "Okay. Where is it?"

"Out on Crescent Lake." She gave Cassidy directions and said she'd meet her there as soon as she could get past the talk she knew was coming from her parents.

"How will you get there?"

"I'll ride my bike."

"No way," Cassidy said. "It's too far, and it's too hot. I'll go to the Dairy Delight, grab a burger and hang out until you show up. Then you can show me where it is, and I'll drive you back to town."

"Okay, but it may be a while."

"Fine. If it's too long and I'm not there, don't

panic and leave. I'll just be cruising around, and I'll be back."

"Okay," Belle said with a nod.

Cassidy put the car in gear. "I'll take you home."

"Drop me off a block from the house, and I'll walk the rest of the way," Belle said. "That way, if both my parents are there, they won't know we've been together."

"Good thinking."

Cassidy did as Belle asked and drove away. She would stop by the drugstore and buy a book she knew she couldn't concentrate on, and then she'd go to the Dairy Delight and wait.

When Belle arrived, her dad's car was in the driveway. Her heart started beating faster. She dreaded the next few minutes. She loved her dad a lot, and he was a good dad. He came to all her dance recitals and softball games. She understood that she shouldn't be angry with him for something that had happened so long ago, especially since she really didn't think he *knew,* but she was uncomfortable nonetheless.

He would be upset about the way she'd run away, and he'd feel like he had to tell her mom what had happened. Belle was afraid her mom would be hurt and mad about what he'd done with Cassidy's mom— so mad that they might fight. She didn't want them to fight. She liked things just the way they were. Why hadn't she just kept her mouth shut and closed the door very quietly behind her?

Heart and footsteps heavy, Belle opened the back door and stepped into the coolness of the kitchen. To her surprise, her mom and dad were sitting at the small breakfast table, talking. They didn't look angry, but they were both frowning.

"Have you called all her friends?" her dad asked.

"Of course I have," her mom said with the barest hint of indignation.

Belle glanced at the key hook by the door. Her uncle's house key was there, just as it always was. She took a deep breath and closed the door. Both her parents turned.

"Belle!" they cried in unison and relief.

Feeling as exposed as if she were standing there stark naked, she forced a feeble smile. "Hi," she said. "Sorry I worried you."

Sophie glanced anxiously at the clock above the kitchen sink. Almost two o'clock and still no sign of Cassidy. There had been no word from Lara Hardisty, either. When Sophie hadn't been able to reach Lara by phone, she'd assumed she was outside with the girls. But the phone call had been placed nearly three hours ago, and Sophie still hadn't heard a word.

She was beginning to worry. If this same thing had happened in Baton Rouge, she wouldn't have been so concerned. She knew all Cassidy's friends and their mothers. *Be truthful, Sophie. Part of the reason you wouldn't be worried is that you would have been so tied up with patients you wouldn't even have known.* Sad, but true. As it was, with her actions limited by her ankle, there wasn't much to do but read magazines, think and watch the clock. She kept thinking about her earlier conversation with Cassidy, and she couldn't get past the idea that something was bothering her. Her smile, as bright as it was, had seemed…forced. She'd seemed nervous, distracted, as if she couldn't wait to get away.

Well, that made two of them. Sophie had decided that it was time to get back to her own life. Time to go home. As she'd told Reed, her usefulness to Donovan was limited, so there was no reason to stay the better part of another week, not with her resistance to Reed so low.

She glanced at the clock for the umpteenth time in as many minutes. Where was Cassidy?

Unexpectedly, as if she'd willed it, she heard the faint sound of an approaching car. Thank goodness! Sophie forced herself to stay seated. If she rushed to the door, demanding to know where Cassidy had been, she would only irritate her daughter.

The car neared, and Sophie frowned. It didn't sound like the Explorer, she thought, as the driver turned off the engine. In seconds she heard the sound of footsteps on the porch—masculine footsteps. Sophie's mouth went dry. If it wasn't Cassidy, then who?

A sudden, sharp rapping at the door caused Sophie to jump. Before she could invite the visitor in, the door opened and Reed stepped inside. Her heart began to pound.

"What are you doing here?" she asked, hearing the sharpness of her voice.

"We need to talk," he said, closing the door behind him and stepping farther into the room.

"I don't think we have anything to say to each other." Sophie strove to maintain a coolness she was light-years from feeling. "Last night—"

"Last night is the least of my concerns right now,"

Reed interrupted. "I want to talk about what happened seventeen years ago."

Sophie sucked in a shocked breath. Was he here to demand his familial right to Cassidy? Though her heart was beating so fast she felt sick, she lifted her chin and said, "You know as well as I do what happened seventeen years ago. You asked me out because you heard I was easy, and I guess I was—for you. You seduced me, and you dumped me when things got too messy for your perfect, rich-boy lifestyle. End of story."

"Is it?" he asked, a muscle in his jaw jumping.

"Oh, excuse me," she added in a sarcastic tone, "I forgot the part where I moved away and tried to put my life back together."

"You forgot something else, didn't you?"

"Like what?"

"Like telling me you were pregnant."

Sophie was so taken aback, she couldn't reply. She wasn't even sure she was breathing. Any thought she might have had of trying to pacify him so that he wouldn't try to claim rights to their daughter vanished beneath an all-consuming fury. What kind of fool did he take her for? And how dare he act as if he didn't know?

"What's the matter, Reed? Have you suddenly found a conscience? Or religion, maybe? Or just a sense of decency?" she asked, struggling to her feet and limping over to where he stood. "Did you see Cassidy and see what a nice kid she is and start thinking about all you've missed and decide you wanted to be a part of her life? How *dare* you!"

Reed looked as if he'd been poleaxed. His eyes

held a dazed expression, and the color had drained from his face. "So it is true?"

"Of course it's true!" Sophie snapped. "You knew perfectly well I was pregnant. When my dad went to see you and your dad the night he d-died—"

"I didn't know, and I never saw your dad the night he died," Reed said, taking advantage of the pause to derail her accusation.

Sophie paid no heed to his denial. All the anguish and outrage and resentment she'd hidden in her heart for so many years came spewing out in a rush of condemnation. "Liar! You told my dad you didn't want any part of me or our baby. You were too young for marriage, and you had college and law school to finish. But that didn't stop you from marrying Lara, did it?"

Dark color suffused Reed's face. He was as furious as she. "I *didn't* know, dammit! And leave Lara out of this. And how can you stand there all filled with self-righteousness after what you threatened to do to me?"

"Threatened?" Sophie spat. "I don't know what you're talking about."

"Rape."

The ugly word hung in the sudden silence like the blade of a guillotine ready to fall. "Rape?"

"Oh, hell," Reed said, throwing up his hands in disgust. "Stop acting so naive. Surely you recall that you and your dad were thinking of slapping a statutory rape charge against me."

"I don't know what you're—" Sophie's thoughts trailed away with a sudden perception. She'd been told one thing; Reed had been told something else. He claimed he didn't know about Cassidy, and unless he was a better actor than she thought he was, there was little doubt from the look on his face that he was telling the truth.

Someone had lied.

Her heart gave a painful lurch. It wasn't hard to figure out who. The wave of comprehension that swept over her left her dizzy and weak. Hutch had said he'd talked to Reed and Rowland, but she knew all too well her father had been wont to spin an elaborate fabrication when the situation warranted. She closed her eyes and shook her head, swaying like saw grass in a stiff ocean breeze.

Sensing that she was about to collapse, Reed slipped an arm around her shoulders. Dazed by her new perception, she looked up at him, and saw that he, too, had come to the same conclusion. Wordlessly he guided her to the rocker she'd just vacated. She sank onto it, and he lowered himself into a nearby armchair. He clasped his hands together, rested his elbows on his knees and leaned forward, staring at the floor.

Painful seconds ticked by. The accusations they'd flung at each other still rang in their ears. Snippets of old conversations and bits and pieces of their youthful encounters played through minds confused by allegations and new understanding. They'd both been lied to. She'd been told he wanted no part of her or the baby she carried; he'd been told she and her father were going to charge him with statutory rape. Lies. Sophie sneaked a glance at Reed. He looked as devastated as she felt.

"It would never have crossed my mind to file any kind of charges against you," she told him in a quiet voice.

"I swear I had no idea you were carrying my baby."

Sophie met his steady gaze and knew he was telling the truth. She'd spent years hating him for abandoning her and Cassidy, and now, it seemed, she'd hated the wrong person. She felt like crying. Like screaming. Like... Like she'd been robbed of something tenuous, precious, something that could never be recaptured or replaced. But those feelings, too, she knew were based on the assumption that things might have been different if Reed had known. Would they have?

"And if you had known?" she asked, needing to know.

"I don't know."

She didn't like the answer, but had to hand it to him for being truthful.

"She knows."

The finality of the statement made Sophie's heart stand still. "Who knows?"

"Cassidy. She overheard you and Donovan talking."

So that's what had been wrong with her when she left. "How...how do you know?"

"She came to my office to confront me about it."

Sophie's mind whirled with questions. Why hadn't Cassidy come to her for verification? Why had she gone to Reed? What must she be thinking? Feeling? "What did she say?"

"She asked me straight out if I was her father. She thought I knew and would validate what she'd heard. I told her the truth. That it was possible."

"How...upset was she?"

"On a scale of one to ten, she was about a nine."

Sophie moaned.

"Look, I think we should put whatever it is that happened between us last night on hold and call a truce until we can work through this."

Sophie nodded. "Where is she? I need to talk to her, to try to explain."

"I don't know where she went," Reed said.

"What do you mean, you don't know where she went? She was supposed to be at Lara's swimming. Oh—" She broke off as understanding dawned. "But that was just something she made up so she could get out of the house to come and see you, wasn't it?"

"Probably. And I meant it when I said I didn't know where she'd gone. While she was at the office, Lara dropped Belle off, so I could take her to lunch. She was outside the door and heard every word Cassidy and I said."

Tears sprang into Sophie's eyes at the enormity of the damage that had been done to two innocent children. "Dear God," she breathed.

"She went running out of the office, and Cassidy followed her. By the time I reached Lara on her cell phone to tell her what was going on, we couldn't find either of them. Luckily, Belle came wandering home about twenty minutes later."

Sophie pushed aside her concern for her own daughter long enough to ask, "Is Belle all right?"

Reed offered Sophie a wan smile. "The kid is truly amazing. I told her the truth as I knew it, omitting some of the parts I didn't think she was old enough to deal with."

"Like my dad's rape charge threat?"

"Exactly. I made no apologies for my actions, but I did tell her I was sorry she and her mother had been hurt by them. Belle is—" he struggled to find the right word "—mature for her age. Aunt Isabelle says she's an old soul. But she seemed fine with the whole thing. She even made a comment about it being cool to have Cassidy for a sister."

With that worry eased, Sophie asked, "Does she know where Cassidy is?"

"She says she doesn't."

"What about Lara?" Sophie asked with a frown of concern. "How did she take the news?"

Reed's reply was as shocking to Sophie as finding out Cassidy knew the truth of her conception. "Lara might have been as surprised as I was to find out that Cassidy is mine, but she's known about you and me from the beginning."

"You're kidding."

"Why?" Reed asked. "Did you keep the truth about Cassidy's paternity from your husband?"

"Of course not!" Sophie denied, stunned that he could even think such a thing. "I could never have done something like that to a man like Jake—to any man for that matter. Jake and his family knew up-front about you and Cassidy. And he couldn't have loved her more if she'd been his."

Sophie saw a flicker of pain in Reed's eyes, but there was nothing she could do about it. Nothing any of them could do to undo the mess her father and his had made of their lives. As painful as regrets for sins might be, the regret for what might have been was even greater.

"I'm glad for that." Reed stood. "Look, try not to worry. Cassidy will show up soon. She's just angry and unhappy right now. Is she in the Explorer?"

Sophie nodded. "Donovan and I will drive into town and look for her."

"No." Reed put a hand on her shoulder. "You stay put in case she comes home. I'm tight with the local law enforcement. I'll have Sheriff Lawrence and the police chief keep a look out for the vehicle. She can't have gone far, and she'll have to face you eventually."

"I suppose so," Sophie said with a nod.

"You know, Aunt Isabelle is right. Your sins do find you out."

"Yes," Sophie said. "They do. Donovan and Jake always told me I should tell Cassidy about you, but I was afraid she'd hate me. Now I suppose she does. Maybe if I'd told her when she was younger she'd have been as accepting as Belle seems to be."

"Maybe," Reed said. "Maybe not. No two kids are the same. Don't beat yourself up about it." He offered her a half smile of encouragement. "Lara and I always say we're doing the best we can as parents, and at least half the time we get it wrong."

Sophie gave a tentative smile in return.

"The good news is that the other half of the time, we're right." Reed reached down and put his finger beneath Sophie's chin, raising it so he could look her in the eye. She felt the reaction deep inside her, even though the timing was all wrong and she knew desire was the last thing she should be feeling at the moment. Still, she couldn't pull away, couldn't bring herself to tell him to stop.

Then he seemed to remember himself and dropped his hand to his side. He left her sitting there and made his way to the door where he turned and said, "I'll call if I hear anything."

When he had gone, Sophie called Donovan inside

to tell him what was going on. She was crying by the time she finished.

"Sounds like Reed's attitude is good," was her brother's comment.

"It was." She shook her head. "I can't believe he didn't know, but knowing Dad's penchant for lying and Rowland's for control, it doesn't surprise me."

"Me neither."

"Can you believe what he said about dad threatening Rowland with a rape charge?"

Donovan stood. "Darlin', if Hutch was involved, I can believe anything." He leaned over, brushed a kiss to the top of her head and started for the door. "Sounds like there's no reason to call out the troops just yet, and I have a lot of work to do. If we don't hear from Reed by suppertime, Jett and I will go looking for Cassidy ourselves."

Sophie nodded. He was halfway out the door when she called his name. He turned, his eyebrows raised in question.

"Thanks," she said.

"For what?"

"For not saying 'I told you so.'"

By the time Reed spoke with Sophie and told her he would ask the sheriff and the police chief to be on the lookout for Donovan's Explorer, it was long gone from the streets of Lewiston. No sooner had Reed left than house than Belle hugged her mother and announced she was going upstairs to watch television. Regarding her daughter with a critical eye and deciding that she didn't seem too upset about the news she'd heard, Lara announced that she was taking a casserole to Aunt Isabelle, whose arthritis was acting up.

Belle told her to go ahead; she'd be fine, and to give Aunt Isabelle a kiss for her. Lara left, thinking that her daughter really was remarkable, and so, for that matter was her ex-husband. Reed had handled his side of the story with delicacy, genuine remorse and a humbleness she knew was based in a sincere fear that his actions might have scarred Belle for life.

Reed Hardisty was a good father and a good man, Lara thought as she carried the casserole to the car. He just wasn't the right man for her. She hoped for his sake and even for Sophie's that they could set aside the hurts of the past and concentrate on making things up to Cassidy. Maybe they could even eke out a future together, if time and circumstance proved there was anything from the past to base a future on. Someone in her family deserved to be happy, and it didn't look as if that were a possibility for either her or her brother.

Belle couldn't believe her luck! She'd wondered how she would manage to escape her mother's eagle eye so she could rendezvous with Cassidy, and then God had answered her prayers in the guise of poor Aunt Isabelle.

Belle watched from her bedroom window as her mother backed out of the driveway. She was out the door and down the stairs in a flash. She filled up the water bottle that went to her bike: the Dairy Delight was clear across town, and the temperatures were soaring. Then, grabbing the key to her uncle Wes's house, she opened the door to the garage, secured the water bottle to the bike and wheeled the ten-speed out into the sunlight.

Ten minutes later Belle rolled into the Dairy Delight parking lot. She was relieved to see the green sports utility vehicle sitting there. She left her bike near the building and went inside. The dimness after the blinding sunshine left her temporarily sightless, and she blinked and squinted and scanned the room's occupants, searching for Cassidy.

"Belle. Over here," Cassidy said, from Belle's left. She blinked again, and finally her eyes began to adjust. Cassidy sat at a booth, the remnants of a cola in a glass, an unopened paperback book open on the table in front of her. Belle hurried across the room and slid into the opposite booth.

"You got here sooner than I expected," Cassidy said.

"My dad—our dad wasn't nearly as long-winded as I expected," Belle said. Then, seeing the dismay on Cassidy's face, she reached out and touched the fist that lay on the book. "I know you're feeling bad right now, Cassidy," she said. "I can't imagine how I'd feel if I were you. I wish I could say something to make you feel better."

"There's nothing you can say. It's just…hard to grasp it all, you know? I mean, my mom lied to me, and my dad, too."

"I know, but they did it to try to keep from hurting you. Which is the exact opposite of the lie my grandfather told your grandfather."

"What was that?"

"My grandpa told your grandpa that when Daddy found out about your mom being pregnant, he said he didn't want either of you. But that was a lie, because Grandpa never told him.''

''Why not?''

''Probably because he didn't really care about your mom. All he was thinking about was my dad and how he wanted him to marry my mom.''

Though Belle hadn't been told the whole truth behind her parents' marriage, she had been told by her mother that the marriage was the wish of both her grandfathers and that she and Reed had been too immature and weak to stand up to them.

The sadness in Cassidy's eyes made Belle's heart ache. ''All I can tell you is that he's really sorry about what happened, and he really wants to make it up to you both.''

''How?''

''I don't know. But he'll figure out something. He's very good at working out problems.'' She glanced at the clock hanging on the far wall and held up the key. ''We'd better get a move on. I need to be back in my room before my mom gets home.''

''Sure,'' Cassidy said, gathering up her book. When they were settled in the car and headed toward the lake house, Cassidy said, ''Are you sure your uncle won't mind if I crash there a day or so?''

''Positive,'' Belle said with a smile. ''And no one will ever find you.''

Chapter Ten

After Reed spoke with the authorities and asked them to be on the lookout for Cassidy's vehicle, he drove straight to his father's office. He knew Rowland's routine, and unless there was an emergency, there were no surgeries scheduled for Monday afternoons. They were long overdue for a showdown—about seventeen years overdue. Reed didn't intend to let another day pass before he confronted his father about his role in the tangle of lies that had deprived him of the knowledge that he'd fathered a child.

He went in the back door of offices whose waiting rooms looked like something you'd see on Fifth Avenue, not Fourth Street. Trudy, a svelte, Nordic-looking divorcée in her forties, who'd been his father's nurse for the past two years and his mistress for a great deal of that time, greeted him with a chilly smile and told him Rowland was with a patient. Trudy knew that Reed knew all about her and his dad.

"I need to see him as soon as he's finished," Reed said.

Her sigh defined her displeasure. "He can't spare but a couple of minutes. He's double booked this afternoon."

"He'll spare whatever time I need, Trudy. I have something very important to discuss with him."

Trudy met his gaze headlong. "And may I tell him what it's about?"

"My daughter."

Concern flickered in her eyes. Rowland doted on Belle. "Is something wrong with Belle?"

Reed, who was already headed down the hall, didn't even deign to answer. "Tell him I'll be in his office."

His father came through the door five minutes later. The expression on Rowland's face was a mixture of irritation and wary concern that deepened to anger when he saw Reed sitting behind his desk.

"What's wrong with Belle?" Rowland asked without preamble.

"There's nothing wrong with Belle."

"Trudy said—"

"That I wanted to talk to you about my daughter," Reed interrupted. "I was referring to Cassidy."

"Cassidy?" Rowland asked. "Who the hell is Cassidy?"

"The daughter I fathered with Sophie Delaney seventeen years ago. You remember? The pregnancy you allegedly talked to me about. The one I supposedly wanted no part of. That pregnancy."

It was a testimony to Rowland's supreme control

that the only indication of his surprise was the briefest darkening of his eyes. "So the little tramp finally told you, did she? Didn't I warn you that she would cause you nothing but pain?"

"My pain has nothing to do with it. Stop trying to cloud the issue," Reed said. "And no, she didn't tell me. Evidently, Cassidy overheard Sophie and Donovan talking. She wanted to find out the truth, so she came to me to corroborate whether or not her mother had lied to her. You can imagine my surprise when she asked me if I was her father."

"Her mother probably put her up to it."

"No, Dad, she didn't. You lied by omission by not telling me Sophie was pregnant. You lied to Sophie about my feelings, and you lied to me about the alleged rape charge, too. When I mentioned that to Sophie, she was as stunned as I was when I learned about Cassidy."

"No." Rowland's answer was as heavy as a stone. "Hutch threatened that, all right. I assumed Sophie was in on it." He sat down in the chair across from his desk. "You may not believe this, but I did what I did out of a concern for you."

Reed's short laugh was hollow, without mirth. "Really?"

"Really," Rowland said, his irritation evident. "What would you have done if you'd known about the baby? Offered to marry her? Hutch Delaney's daughter? You'd have been the laughingstock of the county."

Reed's anger had grown colder and deeper with every malicious word that spewed from his father's mouth. "There are worse things than that."

"Yes, son, there are. Like being saddled with an illiterate drunk's daughter."

"You're incredible, did you know that?" Reed said, amazed at his father's shortsightedness. "Sophie may have been Hutch Delaney's daughter, but you might be surprised to know that not only was she a decent person, she was an honor student," Reed said.

"*I'm* incredible? Good God, man! The girl probably put out for every Tom, Dick and Harry who came along. Did you even stop to consider that the child might not be yours?"

Reed played his trump card. "I'm not—nor was I ever—as stupid or naive as you seem to think. I know Cassidy is mine, Dad, because Sophie was a virgin the one and only time we made love."

Again there was the slightest trace of surprise in Rowland's eyes. "Made love?" He gave a snort of disbelief. "Had sex, you mean. You didn't have enough sense to know the difference."

"Do you?" Reed countered.

"I beg your pardon?"

"What is it with you and Trudy? Not love, I'll bet. You don't know the meaning of the word. So it must be sex."

"Now you just—"

"What, Dad?" Reed challenged. "Stay out of your business? Gladly. If you'll stay out of mine." He stood and went to the door. Turned. "If you want to play God in the operating room, fine. But stay out of my life."

Rowland ignored the directive and asked, "What are you going to do?"

"I don't know," Reed said honestly. "Talk to Sophie and Cassidy and try to come to some sort of peace with this, I guess.''

The smile that settled on Rowland's face could only be described as evil. Reed knew instinctively that he wasn't going to like what he heard next.

''While you're talking, and since you're so insistent on honesty, why don't you ask Sophie what she did with the money.''

Reed's blood ran cold. His fingers tightened on the doorknob. ''What money?''

''The five thousand dollars I gave to Hutch Delaney the night he came to me threatening to have you hauled off to jail for raping his little girl if I didn't—how was it he put it?—'come up with the scratch.' There was no mention of money in any of the police reports, which means someone did something with it.'' He gave another of those chilling smiles. ''And I don't think Donovan took it with him to prison.''

Reed's stomach churned sickeningly.

''You think what I did was interfering in your life, taking over? Call me meddlesome if you will, but there was no way I was going to let you tie yourself to a family like that.''

By the time Donovan and Jett finished for the day, Sophie still hadn't heard from Reed. In desperation she called Lara and was told that she hadn't seen Reed since he left after talking with Belle earlier in the day.

In a trembling voice, Sophie apologized for Belle being hurt inadvertently by Sophie's mistakes. As Reed had, Lara assured Sophie that Belle was taking the news with her customary equanimity. Then Lara took Sophie by complete surprise by saying that she was in no position to cast stones at anyone for what they'd done in their youth.

"Whatever it is that young people feel for one another should never be taken lightly," Lara said. "Age has nothing to do with the depth of emotions, and just because someone is young doesn't mean that what he feels isn't real."

Sophie hung up with a new respect for Lara Hardisty and a question in her mind: was there more to Lara's speech than met the eye? Was she speaking as much about her own youthful feelings for Donovan as she was about Sophie and Reed?

"Who was that?" Donovan asked, coming from the bathroom in a pair of faded jeans, toweling dry his hair.

"Lara."

"What did she say?" His face was hidden by the towel, and the words were muffled, but Sophie heard the tension in them.

"She hasn't heard anything."

Donovan draped the towel around his neck and scraped both hands through his damp hair. "Jett and I will split up and look around a little ourselves. He knows where all the kids hang out. Maybe one of them has seen or heard something."

"Good idea," Sophie said. "What about me?"

"You sit tight. She may come dragging in any minute, and it would be a good idea if you were here if she does."

When Donovan and Jett left, the house seemed unnaturally quiet. There were no sounds of hammering from outside, no *smack, smack* of the pneumatic nail gun, no hip-hop blaring from Jett's boom box, nothing but the sound of Sophie's thoughts that echoed through her mind like sonar bouncing off an unseen object.

Reed. Was there a chance that with the old bitterness and blame behind them they could work together as parents for Cassidy?

Where was she? How was she dealing with the news that Reed was her real father?

Reed and Sophie had hurled some ugly accusations at each other, but as hurtful as the encounter had been, Sophie's training told her that the words needed to be said before the wounds of the past could start to heal.

To give him credit, he'd seemed genuinely upset that her father had planned to charge him with rape and sincere in his regret that he hadn't known about Cassidy. She tried to imagine what it would have been like if he'd said he would marry her, but there was no way she could envision the person she'd been at sixteen as the wife of the more sophisticated nineteen-year-old Reed. Sophie was smart enough to realize that, even if he had chosen to do the right thing, the marriage would a have been doomed from the beginning.

It was better that things turned out as they had. God had given her Jake, who had fulfilled the roles of father and husband the way Sophie could never visualize Reed doing at that age. At nineteen Jake had known exactly who he was and where he was going, something Sophie suspected hadn't come to Reed until much later in life.

There was no hesitation in Reed now. Though she was certain it could go nowhere, he seemed determined to pursue what had happened between them the night before. Sophie was smart enough to know that what they'd experienced was lust, and that desire was never enough for anyone to build a relationship on.

However, now that he'd learned the truth about Cassidy and with their earlier altercation still uppermost on both their minds, Sophie doubted that Reed would want to pursue any kind of relationship with her. Then again, they had cleared the air a bit.

Full circle. Again.

She glanced at the clock, felt a sickening knot of worry curl up in her stomach and forgot Reed, momentarily. The ache in her ankle had nagged at her all day, like the throb of a sore tooth. The uncertainty of Cassidy's whereabouts and the knowledge that she was hurting, too, wore on Sophie's already frayed nerves. She wasn't sure how many more hours of misgivings she could bear without giving in to the anxiety and grief that threatened to overwhelm her. She tried talking to herself, tried giving herself the same advice she would give patients. Somehow when the shoe was on the other foot, the advice didn't seem so wise or so comforting.

Reed didn't know what he hoped to accomplish by facing Sophie with the information about the money. It wasn't a good time, but he needed to see her face when he asked her about it. It wasn't that he begrudged her the money. It was the fact that she hadn't been completely honest with him when she'd had the opportunity.

Reed pulled the car to a stop in front of the Delaney house, went to the door and rapped on the freshly painted wood.

* * *

Certain that it was someone with news about Cassidy, Sophie rose and hobbled to the door. She was taken aback to see Reed standing there. She was more surprised to see that he was angry. Sophie's heart sank. She couldn't do this. She wasn't up for round two with Reed. Not today.

"What is it? What's wrong?" she asked.

"Isn't there something else you forgot to tell me?" He grasped her shoulders and propelled her back inside. Then he closed the door behind them and crossed the room, as if he needed to put some distance between them before facing her.

She started to speak, but he held up a silencing hand.

"Don't bother with the innocent act. I talked to my dad, and he told me all about it."

"Told you all about what?" she asked.

Reed strode back toward her, drawing so close she felt intimidated by his nearness. "That your dad demanded five thousand dollars in exchange for his promise not to go to the police with his lie about my seducing you."

Sophie felt her eyes go wide and the blood drain from her face. *The money. She'd forgotten about the money.*

Reed reached out and tipped back her chin, forcing her to meet the suspicion in his eyes. "What happened to the money, Sophie? There was nothing in the police reports about any money being found on your dad's body or the premises. But a couple of weeks later you up and leave town, and when you come back for your brother's trial you're dressed fit to kill. So I guess you used the money to move up in the world. You bought yourself an education and maybe some respectability and a husband who'd overlook your sins."

Sophie couldn't believe what she was hearing. How could Reed believe that she had anything to do with any extortion plan her dad might have conceived, after the progress they'd made in coming to terms with the lies of the past just this morning? She felt her composure fracture, like a marble left to heat in the oven.

Clinging to the flimsy thread of her self-control, she reached behind her and pulled open the door. "I can't deal with this right now, Reed," she said, trying without success to control the quaver in her voice. "I think you'd better go, before we say things we'll regret."

"We're talking about blackmail, Sophie. My dad said—"

Rowland. The very name set her teeth on edge. She made a low, growling sound, and her brittle grasp on her control broke like a crisp cookie snapped in two. Her face grew hot and the shaking in her hands seemed to possess her entire body.

She was falling apart before his eyes, Reed thought, his concern escalating. He should never have brought up the subject when she had so much on her mind. He cursed his stupidity. He should have waited until they found Cassidy.

"Your *dad* said?" she cried in stark disbelief. "I thought we'd come to the conclusion this morning that *both* our fathers lied to us about what was said when they met to discuss our little mistake. Why would you believe your dad now?"

He held up his hands, palms out. "Forget I asked," he said. "It isn't a good time."

She was trembling like a sail in a capricious breeze, and there was a wild and reckless go-for-broke gleam in her eyes. "You're right, Reed. It's a terrible time. But you brought it up, and now you're going to listen to what I have to say. You want to know if there was money. You're darn right there was money. Lots of money. Not a check. Cash."

"Sophie—"

She ignored him. "When my dad came in that night—very drunk—it was stuffed in every pocket. Hundred-dollar bills, if I remember correctly. But I never suspected it was blackmail money until you told me about this—" she waved a hand in the air "—this rape thing. *His* version of the story was that your dad gave it to him. A little gift so I could go away somewhere, have an abortion and make a fresh start."

Reed made a sound, but Sophie didn't even acknowledge him. She spun around and started to walk as fast as her ankle would carry her, her story trailing out like a ball of twine, full of twists and turns and hopelessly tangled.

"He had his plans for you, and five thousand was probably cheap enough to get me out of your life. Don't forget that Rowland said you had a lot of school to get behind you. God forbid if we cramp the rich boy's lifestyle."

Still pacing, she wrapped her arms around herself, as if she could hold herself together. She threw back her head and laughed, a sound so far from the real thing it was frightening. "My dad was so *proud* of himself for getting something out of you and your dad because you'd 'knocked me up' as he put it."

Reed opened his mouth, but closed it when she came to a halt a scant yard from him. "But I digress. You know all about the money. You're just worried about what happened to it."

For a moment the fire went out of her. She looked around, as if she was disoriented, then she swiped a trembling hand over her face. The feverish intensity in her eyes frightened him, and she was shaking as if she had palsy.

"Donovan came home and—" she swallowed thickly, more in the past than the present "—and my father was…gone, and he told me to hide the money before the police came. He said they'd want to know what it was for, and everyone would know about me…and the baby. He said that if I stayed in Lewiston, I'd wind up like Mama. I didn't want to take it, but I did what he said."

Reed reached out to her. She jerked away from him. "Don't touch me!" She stood there breathing hard. Finally she continued. "Then, in a few days, I got a call from your dad, telling me to keep the money."

"My dad called you?" Reed asked, incredulous.

Her tears fell faster, and she looked at him with anger and defiance burning in her blue eyes. "You want to know if I took the money. Damn right I did. Did I use it to buy some clothes? Yes. I didn't want to come back to town with my tail tucked between my legs, so Jake married me, and he came with me, so you and your dad wouldn't know how much I'd been hurt.

"Did I use the money for my education? Why shouldn't I have? I had a baby to raise—alone, I thought. But do you want to know about my real education? The one from the school of hard knocks? That went on twenty-four hours a day, seven days a week, year in, year out?''

Sophie paused for breath. Reed prayed that she'd stop, but it was as if now that she'd started, she wouldn't quit until she'd regurgitated all the hard feelings and anger she'd been holding in.

''I know it must have been hard, but—''

''Hard?'' She made a noise, something between a growl and a groan, and, raising her fists, she struck his chest. ''Damn you!'' she said, hitting him again. ''You don't know the meaning of hard!''

Reed tried to grab her hands, which was more difficult than it looked. She managed to land several painful blows before he snared one wrist. Immediately her other fist smacked the crest of his cheekbone. He snagged her other wrist. She was breathing as if she'd just finished a five-kilometer run, but she still fought to be free. When she realized she was getting nowhere, she stopped, and a dead calm took control of her features. Reed wasn't sure which was more disturbing—her ranting and raving or the emptiness in the eyes that looked at him.

''Jake and I lived in a one-bedroom apartment and paid our way through school,'' she said, her gaze focused inward, on memories of the past. ''We waited tables, and we worked our jobs and our classes around Cassidy, so that one of us would be with her all the time. And I held her in one arm while I wrote with the other. I wore clothes from the Salvation Army so she could have pretty things.

''And guess what? While you were out playing the hotshot on campus, squiring around cheerleaders and sorority snobs, having a fine old time of it, Jake Carlisle was right beside me, rocking her when she had colic and sharing the load that was rightfully yours. And he never complained, Reed. Not once.''

The last of the anger faded with the declaration, and the last of the starch leached from her bones. She collapsed against him with a heart-wrenching sob. His arms closed around her as the tears started afresh. Even then, she fought him, landing a couple of half-hearted, ineffective blows to his back.

Reed wasn't sure when he'd seen so many tears. Surely not since three weeks after his marriage to Lara, when she'd lost the baby she'd been carrying. Now, as he had then, Reed felt totally incompetent to deal with the situation.

Sophie's tears wet the front of his shirt. Needing the comfort of human contact, she burrowed closer. Now, as he had with Lara, he tried the only thing he knew to do: he whispered that it would be okay, and oh, God, he was sorry…sorrier than she'd ever know. Sophie cried even harder.

He told himself that the tears were a catharsis, good for her, but after the depth of her emotional outburst, he wasn't so sure. He held her close, his hands moving over her back, smoothing, stroking, comforting as best he could, while his lips moved over her temples, the corners of her eyes and her tear-wet cheeks, sipping the salty moisture with a tenderness he didn't even recognize, and brushing away the tears with the gentle sweep of his thumbs.

Somehow, during his ministrations, his mouth found the corner of hers, and for some reason Sophie turned into the kiss. Filled as it was with so many long-pent-up emotions, the impact was explosive. Reed felt the shock all the way to his soul. There was desperation in the kiss, hunger, sorrow and a need to blot away the memories of the past and replace them with new ones.

Her lower body arched against him and he filled his hands with warm feminine flesh. She moaned, and the sound of her pleasure released a low growl of satisfaction from his throat. It seemed their hands were everywhere, that the kisses grew deeper and wilder, yet neither of them seemed to be in any hurry. It was as if, remembering their awkward, youthful coupling, they both wanted to savor every second of satisfaction, to drink every drop of desire.

She felt so right in his arms. So good. And something about having her there made Reed feel complete. He tempered the driving urge to lower her to the floor and take her before either of them could think of some reason they shouldn't. But he held back, accepting his cue from her, offering her no reason to come back to him later with blame.

This time he wanted to do it right.

Sophie's intellect told her she was crazy. Her heart whispered that it didn't matter. She didn't have the strength to try and figure out which part of her was right. If she'd been thinking straight, she'd have known there would be remorse later, but at that moment she was only feeling, acting on impulse, guided by a need as ancient and elemental as breathing.

For hours, it seemed, Reed's lips had moved over her face, teasing her with soft half kisses that just missed her lips and taunted her with the promise of desire. Finally, for some reason she would never be able to fathom, she'd ended her misery and turned her mouth to his.

Liberated by the venting of seventeen years' worth of bad feelings and filled with an urgency she had no desire to understand, she ran her palms over the front of his shirt, sliding her hands up to clasp his neck.

For aeons they traded kiss for drugging kiss. His mouth was as delicious as she'd remembered from the night before. Just as seductive, just as dangerous. But for the first time since she'd made love with Reed seventeen years ago, Sophie didn't care about danger or recriminations or consequences. All she cared about was his next kiss, of the way he coaxed her lips apart with gentle persuasion, nibbling, licking, igniting a burning need deep inside her. All she cared about was forgetting....

She cradled his face between her palms. The feel of his end-of-day stubble was as arousing as his body that was pressed so close she could feel every masculine line of him as well as the rapid beating of his heart. It wasn't enough. As the stroking of his tongue grew deeper and their caresses more intimate, she felt a feverish need to get nearer still.

"Sophie?" It was a question. A caress.

He wanted to know if it was all right. Sophie's answer was to slide her hands from his neck to his shirtfront, where she began to undo the buttons. Reed was so still he might have been a statue but for the breath that tickled the tendrils of hair falling over her forehead.

The shirt undone, she made a tactile exploration of his chest, reveling in the feel of firm muscle, taut flesh and wiry hair against her palms. She leaned forward and pressed a kiss to his chest, breathing in the scent of soap and cologne and warm, exciting male.

Reed sucked in a sharp breath. It was as if the

single act snapped the tenuous hold he had on his control. Without a word he scooped her up in his arms and carried her into the hall, stopping only long enough to ask her which bedroom was hers. Inside he tossed her gently onto the softness of the bed. She reached up for him, but instead of lowering himself beside her, he pulled off his shirt and shed all of his clothes except his silk boxers.

He was beautiful all firm flesh and gold-dusted hair. As she struggled with her bemusement, he reached down and peeled her T-shirt over her head, then stripped off her shorts. He pinned her to the crisp sheets, one leg on either side of her body. As he lowered his head to kiss her, Sophie tried and failed to read the emotion in his eyes.

The kiss was sweet, fleeting, and Sophie's hand came up to hold his head closer. "Please," she moaned against his mouth, the nails of her free hand digging into his back. She expected him to kiss her again; instead, he flicked the front clasp of her bra. Nothing stood between her bare breasts and him but the heat in his eyes. Soon there was nothing.

Slowly and deliberately he meshed his fingers with hers and pinned her hands to the bed just above her head. His gaze feasted on her body while Sophie melted in a slow burn. Just when she thought she would go crazy if he didn't kiss her, he lowered his body into hers. Then, palm to palm, heart to heart, mouth to mouth, they raced to the edge of ecstasy....

Later. Much later.... Sophie's small body lay nestled in Reed's arms, their legs twined around each other like vines to a trellis, while the cool breath of the air-conditioning dried the perspiration from their bodies and their heartbeats slowed to a lazy cadence.

With the return of sanity and rational thought, Reed contemplated the next step in their relationship. As rife as it was with the complications of the past, accepting responsibility for his actions didn't seem like the gargantuan undertaking it had felt like at nineteen. Growing older and gaining experience and wisdom was good for perspective if nothing else, he thought. No matter what might happen, he was more determined than ever to give himself and Sophie a chance to see if they had a future. And he knew that if they hoped to build a life together, it would have to start with him and his attempts to make amends for his past actions. That, and establishing a relationship with his daughter.

He tightened his hold on Sophie and pressed a kiss to her forehead. "I'm sorry I flew off the handle without knowing the whole story. I had no idea you'd been through so much."

"Words are cheap," she said, pulling free and moving away from him.

Reed was stunned by her sudden about-face.

"How long will you believe me this time, Reed?" she asked, shoving her hair away from her tear-stained face in an angry gesture that lifted her shapely breasts. "Until Rowland tells you another half-truth?"

He knew he deserved it, but not now, not after the completely satisfying lovemaking they'd shared. "What the Sam Hill is the matter with you?" he snapped. "One minute you're curled up in my arms purring with satisfaction because—correct me if I'm wrong—we engaged in some pretty fantastic lovemaking. The next minute you're throwing nasty comments around. I'm having a hard time figuring out which is the real you," he said, unable to keep the sarcasm out of his voice.

Sophie's hands curled into fists. They sat there on the bed, naked and glaring at each other.

"You don't get it, do you?" she said, crystalline tears forming in her blue eyes. "My daughter is missing, God knows where, hurting because of a mistake I made. I should be out there looking for her, but no! What do I do? I go to bed with the same man and make the same mistake all over again."

Reed's initial reaction was to say that it wasn't a mistake, but something kept him quiet while he digested what she'd just said. On the surface, it sounded like bitter recriminations, another slap in the face; on a deeper level he realized that the anger was based in guilt. He saw what had happened between them as a new beginning, Sophie must see it as history repeating itself. But now wasn't the time to try to convince her otherwise. Now was the time to try to help her get past her blame.

"I'm not a moron. I understand more than you think. Don't do this to yourself," he begged in a soft voice. "Don't do this to me."

"Don't do what?"

"Throw away the past hour because of some misguided sense of guilt."

"Misguided?" she said, her voice filled with anguish. "There's nothing misguided about it. I know what I did, Reed, what we did, and—"

"So do I," he interrupted. He reached out and took her shoulders in a firm grip. "You were raw and hurting, bleeding inside, and you needed some comfort. I was here, and I gave it to you. Don't begrudge me that. I should have been there to comfort you back then."

Her eyes searched his. He let all his feelings show. The regret. The sorrow. The hope.

For long seconds she didn't say anything. "It's easy to say the right things when you're in a bedroom in a house in the woods," she said at last. "It's something else to say them when they're apt to cause an uproar."

Reed saw the statement as a not-so-subtle reminder that he hadn't owned up to their relationship in the past. Another jab he deserved. While he thought about how best to answer, he got up and began to dress.

"You're right," he said, pulling on his shorts, "and I think that's what's at the root of our problem, here. You still feel something for me, but a part of you resents me for not being there for you. I don't blame you for that. I have no excuse except that I didn't know about Cassidy. But if I hadn't avoided you, maybe I would have known."

He retrieved his slacks from the floor. "One of Aunt Isabelle's favorite expressions is 'If you want to dance you have to pay the fiddler.' I think you feel as if we both danced, but you were the only one who paid." His lips twisted in a wry smile. "Not true. I'm just paying later, that's all. And it seems to me that a lot of penalties and interest have accrued through the years."

Sophie looked as if she wanted to say something, then changed her mind and pressed her lips together.

"If it's any consolation, you weren't just another conquest for me," he told her, shoving the tail of his shirt into his slacks. "I did care about you. But being the first is a pretty heavy load for a guy, at least it was for me. I was confused about what I felt for you, but I was smart enough to know I wasn't ready for any kind of commitment. I certainly wasn't ready for marriage.''

He blew out a harsh breath, but the expression in his eyes was tender. ''I'm grateful you found Jake Carlisle, Sophie. I'm happy that Cassidy had him for a father. He sounds like a heck of a guy, and I envy him for what he had with you.''

Sophie made no reply, and Reed reached for his socks. ''So here we are. Déjà vu all over again, as they say. I can't change my actions in the past. I made a mess of things back then by not following my heart. Don't you do the same thing because you have.''

''What do you mean?'' she asked, speaking for the first time in several seconds.

''I think that what happened between us just now happened only partly because you were hurting. I think the real reason is you wanted me as much as I wanted you, and now you're feeling guilty. It seems to me that the way most of us counteract guilt is to run as far away as we can—which is what I did—or hide it with anger. The old fight-or-flight dilemma. But neither avenue works for long. In the end we've got to face a situation squarely and figure out the best course of action.''

Chapter Eleven

Reed left soon after delivering his final salvo. His parting words rankled, especially since Sophie *was* feeling so guilty. Still, she knew he was right. She was angry with herself for falling into bed with him, and she did feel a certain amount of resentment because he'd been spared any responsibility for their youthful indiscretion.

But understanding didn't assuage her guilt for letting history repeat itself. She should have been looking for Cassidy, not making love with Reed. Her only excuse was that once she'd purged herself of all the old hurts and negative feelings, she'd been empty and looking to reclaim herself. She'd wanted to lay down the load of sorrow and responsibility she'd carried alone for so long and feel like a woman again.

She'd desperately needed to forget it all—what had happened in the past what might happen in the future and all the problems connected to both. Just once, she'd wanted to live for the moment, to be selfish and cater to her own needs. Needs. Oh, she'd had them. She'd needed to be filled with new life, new feelings. She needed to feel cherished and comforted. To feel…

When Reed had held her and kissed her, the self-consciousness she'd experienced the night before was gone, vanished along with the bitter memories and misconceptions of the past. And it had just…happened.

Sophie stepped into the shower and ducked her head beneath the spray. She was older, smarter, wiser than she had been at sixteen. She'd once given not only her body but all the love in her young heart to Reed Hardisty, hoping against hope for some sort of miracle that would change her life. Hoping Reed would be her white knight.

This time she had no intention of deluding herself. What had happened was a moment out of time. It would take them nowhere. She'd forgotten, she'd satisfied needs, she'd laid down her load for just a little while. She'd been fine with that an hour ago. Now, in retrospect, it wasn't enough. Still, she knew it would have to suffice. It was time to pick up the load, carry the responsibility. Live with the regrets. Regrets she knew would last a lifetime.

Donovan returned alone. Neither he nor Jett had any luck locating Cassidy. It was, he said, a grim expression on his face, as if she'd vanished from the face of the earth.

At that, Sophie broke into fresh tears, and Donovan could have kicked himself for his poor choice of words. She told herself that the chance of something sinister happening to Cassidy was small, but common sense told her it could happen.

In desperation, on the off chance that Cassidy had escaped to some place where she might feel more secure, Sophie called their condo in Baton Rouge and left a message on the machine, begging her daughter to stay put until she got there so they could talk.

Darkness fell, and with it more tears. Donovan spoke with Reed, who said he'd called in every marker owed him and had everyone looking who might possibly be able to find out any bit of information. It never occurred to Sophie to ask what reason he was giving to the authorities for his interest in the search for Sophie Delaney's daughter.

Cassidy was uncomfortable in the house by the lake, which was built and furnished like a mountain lodge, very rustic and masculine. When she'd first arrived, she'd whiled away an hour or more exploring the two-bedroom house and peeking at Wes Grayson's art. She'd been surprised to find a seminude painting of a redheaded woman who, despite the bold, Impressionistic strokes, bore an uncanny resemblance to her aunt Justine. Something about the lazy, provocative look in the woman's eyes had left Cassidy with an uncomfortable feeling. She'd left Wes Grayson's studio unable to shake the notion that she'd poked her nose in somewhere she shouldn't have.

Feeling sorry for herself, feeling like a burglar or something, she cried herself to a fitful sleep and woke more depressed than before. She watched a cable movie—or tried to. It was hard when the conversation she'd overheard between her mother and uncle kept churning through her mind, like an ESPN instant re-play. Had it been less than twelve hours since she'd found out the truth about her father?

Her father. Reed Hardisty. Now that she'd had time to get used to the idea, she realized she was more upset because she'd been lied to than because of her mother's behavior. Her mom would have been her age when she got pregnant, something Cassidy had always known on some level, but hadn't wanted to look at too closely. Looking meant facing the fact her mother had feet of clay.

Cassidy wondered how her mom felt about Reed now. A better question might be how she herself felt about him. She gave the question some serious thought. She'd liked him well enough before...when she'd thought of him as Belle's dad. He was good-looking and he seemed nice, but she couldn't imagine him and her mom having sex. She hadn't thought about her mom and sex when her dad—Jake—was alive. Their sleeping together was something that just *was*.

Cassidy's stomach growled and she realized she hadn't had anything since the cereal she'd eaten before she left her uncle's house that morning. She'd been too upset to eat the burger she'd ordered at the Dairy Delight. She plundered the contents of Wes Grayson's refrigerator, leaving a five-dollar bill under the empty fruit bowl on the counter as payment, and ate her dinner and cried while she listened to someone called Billie Holiday on Wes Grayson's CD player. The woman's bluesy voice and the haunting words fit her mood, and Cassidy found herself wanting nothing more than to go home.

As angry and hurt as she was, she loved her mom,

and she knew her bad feelings would pass. She thought about what a worrier her mom was. Racked with a sudden, sharp pang of guilt, Cassidy reached for the phone book and looked up Belle's number. She would check with Belle and see if she'd heard how her mom was doing. Cassidy punched in the Hardistys' number, but no one answered. She hung up without leaving a message.

The hoot of an owl drew her gaze toward the French doors that led to the deck. Some other creatures were making a racket, and she thought she heard the howling of a dog. It was growing dark, and with no streetlights, the cabin would be pitch-black. Cassidy couldn't remember if there was any moon or not. It wasn't that she was afraid to stay by herself, but this was a strange place, isolated from neighbors....

She pulled the plaid drapes and went back into the combined living-dining area, her feet dragging. Her heart told her she should get in the Explorer and go home, but as miserable as she was, she couldn't find the courage to do so.

Belle and her mother went to the Dairy Delight for dinner. Lara was picking at a taco salad, and Belle was working on a large cheeseburger and fries basket, but her appetite seemed to be on vacation somewhere. Of all the places in the café, her mom had chosen the booth where Belle and Cassidy had sat earlier, planning Cassidy's escape. Guilt sat as heavily on Belle's mind as the greasy fries did in her churning stomach.

"Are you feeling okay?" her mother asked, a frown drawing her dark eyebrows together.

Belle pushed the half-eaten burger aside. "I'm not very hungry."

Lara reached across the table and laid the back of her hand against Belle's forehead. She closed her eyes so she wouldn't have to look at the concern on her mother's face.

"What's wrong?" The sound of her dad's voice sent Belle's eyes flying open.

"I think she's trying to get sick," Lara said.

Belle's dad slipped into the booth beside her and tipped her chin up so he could take a good look at her. "She does look a little peaked. What's the matter kiddo?"

"I'm just not hungry," Belle said, reaching for her cola.

Lara shrugged. "Has anyone heard from Cassidy yet?"

Belle's dad shook his head and raked his fingers through his hair. The despair and worry in his eyes made her want to cry.

"Sophie's worried sick. So am I. I've asked the city police and the sheriff's office to look around unofficially, but no one remembers seeing her, and Explorers that color are a dime a dozen in Lewiston."

"What can we do?"

"I don't know. Sophie is convinced she's been kidnapped or something."

"Kidnapped!" Belle said, surprised by the idea. "Why does she think that?"

"Because she thinks she'd have come home before now to talk things out."

"Oh."

Belle's dad, who looked years older than he had yesterday, took her face between his palms and said, "Promise me that if anything as important as this ever comes up with the three of us, that you won't go off and upset your mother and me this way."

Belle nodded. Her throat felt as if something were stuck in it, and tears stung her eyes. "Promise," she said in a whisper.

"We don't mean to scare you, punkin'," Lara's mom said, 'but when you're a parent and something is wrong with one of your kids, it can be terrifying."

Belle nodded again.

"Are you eating?" her mom asked her dad. "I see the waitress."

He shook his head. "I couldn't force it down. Damn! Where can she be?"

Belle kept her eyes glued to the plastic tablecloth. *Please, dear God. Let us go home.* In a few minutes her dad announced he was leaving, and she and her mom followed him out. When Belle hugged him goodbye, she clung to him and whispered, "I'm sorry."

He smiled. "Hey," he said softly, chucking her beneath the chin. "It's not your fault."

Belle tried to smile back. She knew that it was.

The first thing Belle's mom did when she got home was check the caller ID. "Oh, good. Your uncle Wes is home."

"Oh, no!" Belle cried, as a light-headed feeling swept through her. Was Cassidy still there? Had he found her? Then rational thought returned, and she realized Cassidy must have tried to call. At least she *hoped* that was what had happened.

Her mom looked shocked by the outburst. "Why are you so upset about Uncle Wes coming home?"

"I'm not upset," Belle said, striving to keep her

voice calm and nonchalant. She'd have to call Cassidy and tell her not to call anymore because of the caller ID. "I guess I was just…surprised. I thought he was going to be gone for a couple of weeks."

"Well, obviously, he changed his mind. Are you sure you're okay, honey? Should I have Grandpa Rowland come over and take a look at you?"

"No!" She softened her voice. "I'm fine."

Though her grandfather spoiled her terribly, Belle had a sneaking suspicion that he was still mad at her mom and dad for getting a divorce, and he was so bossy. He expected her to be perfect. Besides, she had to go call Cassidy and tell her what was going on. Or—Belle had a terrible thought—what if her Uncle Wes had already discovered the intruder in his house?

"I think I'll go take a bath and watch some TV," she said. "Maybe it'll make me feel better."

"Good idea," her mom said, but she was looking at her with that same worried expression Belle had seen in her dad's eyes.

Belle was halfway up the stairs when the image of her dad's face—all sad and worried—rose before her again. *It's not your fault.* She went to her knees on the stairs, and tears started rolling down her cheeks. Big fat tears and deep racking sobs. She hated lying to her parents. And wasn't it lies that had started all this mess with her dad and Cassidy and her mom?

Without stopping to think about what Cassidy would say, Belle stood and ran back down to the kitchen. When she got there, her mom was hanging up the phone.

"That's funny," she said, a puzzled expression on her face. "I called Wes and some woman answered. When I asked to speak to him, she hung up." Then, seeing Belle's tears, she said, "Honey! What is it? What's wrong?"

"That isn't some woman, and Uncle Wes isn't at home."

"Belle, what on earth are you talking about? I just spoke to her. I know she's there."

"It isn't a woman," Belle insisted. "It's Cassidy."

By the time Reed came over and they got the whole story from Belle, she'd calmed down some, but she kept repeating "I'm sorry," over and over. Both Reed and Lara assured her that it was okay, that she was just doing what she thought was best. Reed wanted to call Sophie, but Belle told him she needed to talk to him—in private. Meeting Lara's eyes over Belle's head, Reed agreed. Lara went up to run Belle's bath, something she hadn't done in at least six years, giving them the privacy Belle had requested.

"What is it, sweetheart?" Reed asked, reaching out and taking Belle's cold hand in his.

"I'm trying to understand what happened."

"I know you are, but I'm not sure you're going to until you're older."

"Did you love Sophie when you…you know?"

Reed thought about that. Now wasn't the time to lie. "I'm not sure. I had feelings for her that I didn't understand. I think that maybe it was love, as much as I knew how to love back then."

"What do you mean?"

Reed heaved a deep sigh. "Your understanding of what real love is changes as you grow older. You feel strongly about things as teenagers, but as you get older your perceptions change and you look at people and experiences differently. Do you see what I'm getting at?''

''Not really,'' Belle said, a look of concentration drawing her dark eyebrows together. ''What about now? Do you love her now?''

Reed chose his words carefully. ''I still have feelings for her, and I think it's love—or could be—but we aren't the same people we were as kids. We don't know each other as grown-ups. We'd have to get to know each other and see if what we feel will turn into love.''

Belle nodded. ''Don't people get married because they love each other?''

''Of course they do.''

''Did you love Mom when you got married? And did you get a divorce because you fell out of love with her?''

Leave it to Belle to ask the hard questions. Reed wasn't sure how to handle that one. Finally he said, ''There are all kinds of love, sweetheart. Your mom and I both had feelings for other people when we got married, but we were both hurting, and we let ourselves be talked into marriage by Grandpa Rowland and Grandpa Phil. It's called being on the rebound.''

As usual, Belle focused on the one thing Reed wished he hadn't mentioned.

Belle's eyes widened in surprise. ''Mom loved someone else? Who?''

''She'd been dating someone else, someone Grandpa Phil didn't approve of, I suspect, but I don't know who, and that's the truth. Your mother is a very private person. And I wouldn't ask her about it, if I were you, because it might still be painful for her.''

Belle nodded in understanding.

"You asked if I loved her when we got married, and I said there were different kinds of love. To answer your question, yes. I loved her. I still love her. I liked her very much, and I respected her, but I wasn't *in love* with her. And I think if you ask her, she'll say the same thing about me. And we didn't get a divorce because we fell out of love, we got the divorce because it wasn't the right kind of love. We do care for each other, Belle. Very much. We decided it wasn't fair to stay married to each other when there might be someone out there we could be in love with."

Belle shook her head. "I don't get it."

Reed patted her hand and smiled. "I know. But you will. In time. Any more questions?"

Belle shook her head again.

"Then if you're okay, I need to call Sophie and go get Cassidy." He stood to go to the phone.

"Dad?"

"Yes, sweetheart?"

"If you and Sophie get to know each other and decide you love each other, will you get married?"

Reed felt as if someone had knocked the wind out of him. It was a scenario he hadn't let himself think about, and it was way too early too make that call, especially since he had so much making up to do with Sophie. "I don't know, Belle. We'll have to wait and see."

Sophie was sitting at the kitchen table talking to Donovan when the phone rang. Donovan answered it and handed the receiver to Sophie, mouthing "Reed."

"Reed!" she said eagerly. "What is it? Have you heard something?"

"Yeah," he said. "Belle came clean. Cassidy is at Wes's place out on the lake. Belle knew where she was all this time, but she didn't want to tell because she said Cassidy needed some space. When she saw how worried we all were, her conscience got the best of her and she confessed."

"So she's out at the old Grayson cabin?" Sophie asked, unable to control her excitement.

"Yes."

"Thanks, Reed. Donovan and I are leaving right now," Sophie said.

"Let me."

"What?"

"Let me go. I think it's important for me to talk to her, explain my side." His short laugh filtered through the phone lines. "Now that I know more about my side. I want her to understand that I didn't know, and I think she should be looking at me eye to eye when I tell her."

Sophie's heart beat out a slow, tortured rhythm. She knew Reed was right, that Cassidy needed to hear his side of the story and that her own conversation with her daughter could wait. But letting Reed acknowledge himself as Cass's dad also meant relinquishing a piece of her to someone else.

When she didn't reply immediately, he said, "God knows we've made a mess of things. *I've* made a mess of things. After today I think you and I have hurt each other about all we can, but as much as I can, I want to make what I did right. I want to be there for Cassidy if she'll let me. If you'll let me."

There it was. The thing Sophie feared the most was

out in the open. Reed wanted to be part of Cassidy's life, which led automatically to her second greatest fear: that somehow he might take Cassidy away from her. Still, he had owned up to his culpability, and she had to admire him for being willing to try to make amends. She had no choice but to grant him his request.

"All right," she said, her voice thick with tears. "Go. We'll wait here."

"I hear reluctance in your voice, Sophie, and I think I know why. But you need to remember one thing."

"What's that?" she asked in a barely audible whisper.

"I'm not my dad."

Cassidy was watching a made-for-TV movie, thinking that she'd made a terrible mistake in calling Belle. Cassidy hadn't thought of the Hardistys having caller ID, and she certainly hadn't expected Lara Hardisty to think that her brother had come home and call him back.

She saw the lights of a vehicle coming down the rutted lane and ran to the door. Who could it be? Wes Grayson? What should she do? What reason could she tell him for her being in his house?

Another thought hit her. Maybe it was a prowler who'd found out Wes was gone and had come to steal the family silver. She sneaked another peek. Whoever it was had stopped the car and was coming up the walk to the porch. A man! Cassidy jumped back into the shadow next to the door and held her breath.

Knuckles rapped on the door. Her breath eased out

slowly. A prowler wouldn't knock. Wes Grayson would have a key. Then who—

"It's Reed, Cassidy."

Reed!

"Belle told us you were here—"

The little squealer!

"—so come on. Open the door. Your mother is worried sick about you, and running away won't help any of us. We need to talk. Like adults."

Cassidy blinked back tears. She could almost see her mom—pacing, wringing her hands, crying.... She closed her eyes. Reed was right. Sooner or later she was going to have to deal with the facts. Sooner or later she was going to have to talk to her mom, and she was going to have to face the man standing outside Wes Grayson's door, pleading with her. Slowly she reached out and unlocked the door.

The sound of the dead bolt clicking was one of the sweetest sounds Reed had ever heard. He opened the door and stepped inside, flipping on the light as he entered.

Cassidy blinked in the sudden brightness. She looked tired, he thought, and she seemed nervous. But the anger he'd seen in her eyes that morning had been replaced by wariness.

"Does my mom know I'm here?" she asked.

He nodded. "I called her."

Cassidy looked surprised. "Why didn't she come?"

"She was going to, but I thought you and I needed some time to talk. I don't think we finished this morning, did we?"

She shook her head.

"Why don't we sit down," Reed suggested. "What I have to say is pretty heavy stuff."

"Sure," she said with a shrug.

He followed her to the kitchen table and pulled out a chair across from hers. She looked at him, waiting for him to make the first move. Reed, whose courtroom experience stood him in good stead in most tense situations, felt a trickle of perspiration slide down his spine.

"I'm going to be honest with you about some things, Cassidy. I'm going to tell you some things your mother may not want you to know. But I think you ought to know the whole truth, so you'll understand better how this all came about."

Reed thought about how complicated the tale was and how he and Sophie were having a hard time grasping the duplicity of both their fathers. To expect Cassidy to comprehend the tangle of lies was almost more than he could hope.

"I can handle it," she said.

Reed nodded. "This morning you asked me if I was your father, and I said I didn't know, but that it was possible. That was the truth. But I spoke with your mother—twice, in fact—and it seems that it is true."

A spark of Cassidy's earlier anger glittered in her eyes. "You're saying you didn't know?" she said. "But how could you not know?"

"Your mother never told me," Reed explained. "From what she and I have been able to piece together from what we were told back then, her dad found out and went to talk to my dad."

Cassidy's face wore a look of rapt attention.

"When your grandfather came home, he told your

mother that he spoke to my father and me, which isn't true. I knew nothing about the meeting or what was said there until today. Evidently, my dad told your grandfather that I wanted no part of Sophie or her baby. I was told that your grandfather threatened to have me thrown into jail for statutory rape—I was nineteen, and your mom was only sixteen—if he wasn't given five thousand dollars.''

Cassidy drew in a sharp breath. ''That's black-mail.''

''Any way you cut it,'' Reed said with a nod. ''When I confronted Sophie about that, she said that yes, her dad came home with the money, but his version of the story was that my dad gave it to him so she could get an abortion and start a new life some-where.''

Cassidy's mouth fell open.

''Do you want to hear the rest?'' Reed asked. ''It gets pretty ugly.''

''I want to know everything,'' Cassidy said, raising her chin in determination.

''When your mom told your grandpa she wouldn't have the abortion, he…hit her.''

''He what?''

Reed nodded. ''She already had cracked ribs from the beating she took when he found out she was preg-nant.'' Reed had gleaned that information from the newspaper years ago. The facts had been part of Don-ovan Delaney's defense argument. Cassidy's eyes filled with tears.

''Anyway, your Uncle Donovan came home and tried to stop him. When your grandfather came after him, Donovan took the shotgun down and…used it.

He said if he hadn't your grandfather would have killed her—maybe them both.''

"She never told me," Cassidy said, shaking her head and dislodging the tears that trickled down her pale cheeks. "I knew Uncle Donovan had gone to jail for shooting Granddad, but I never really knew any of the details. Mom always said that Granddad was drunk, and it was a mistake. I always assumed it was one of those gun accidents you hear about.''

"I know this is a lot for you to digest, especially the part about your grandfather. Believe me, your mom and I have had our share of surprises today, too. We're still trying to sort things out.''

Cassidy looked pensive. "I never gave any thought to the fact that if it was an accident, Uncle Donovan wouldn't have had to go to jail." She raised a defensive gaze to Reed's. "My granddad must have done what Uncle Donovan claimed, because he'd never hurt a fly," she said in her uncle's defense. "He's the most gentle man I know...next to my dad." Her gaze flew to Reed's. "I mean Jake.''

Reed didn't say anything, and Cassidy asked, "What happened to the money?''

"She took it and moved to Louisiana and used it to help get an education so she could provide for you," he said, passing on what Sophie had told him and knowing as he did that it was the truth and that she had nothing to be ashamed of.

"And that's where she met...Jake." It was as much a question as a statement.

Reed nodded. "I think you were right before, Cassidy," he told her. "That's where she met your dad. It takes more than being there at conception to be a father. I wasn't there for your mom or you, and I can say in all honesty that I'm grateful that you both had Jake Carlisle.''

Cassidy looked at him with tear-glazed eyes. ''So am I,'' she said, and when Reed's heart broke just the slightest bit, he knew he was feeling the first twinges of love—and a father's jealousy.

''I'm not Jake, Cassidy,'' he told her. ''I have a temper and sometimes I get too wrapped up in my work. I've made my share of mistakes with Belle. What you had with Jake Carlisle was very special. I could never take his place, and I wouldn't want to. What I'm asking is for you to give me a chance to make my own place in your life.''

The tears in Cassidy's eyes spilled over her lashes and down her cheeks. She caught her lower lip in her teeth to still its trembling and gave a single nod.

Reed felt his heart expand in another burst of love. He knew he didn't deserve this beautiful, vibrant and obviously sensitive young woman's love, and also that he would do anything in his power to earn it.

Chapter Twelve

Sophie was waiting at the door when Reed and Cassidy pulled up in separate vehicles. She hurried outside, across the porch and down the steps, taking Cassidy in a crushing embrace that she returned just as fervently. Reed joined Donovan inside, giving mother and daughter the privacy they needed.

"I'm sorry I worried you," Cassidy said, tears streaming down her cheeks.

Battling her own tears, Sophie hugged Cassidy tighter, then held her at arm's length. "I'm the one who's sorry. I was supposed to be setting the example, Cass, and I was afraid that if I told you the truth about Reed you'd think I was a hypocrite." She managed a watery smile. "Now I suppose you think I am anyway."

"No," Cassidy said, wiping at her tears with her

fingertips. "I think you made a mistake. I just hope you'll remember that when I make mine."

"Just don't make the same ones," Sophie cautioned. She hugged Cassidy close, and together they moved toward the porch where they sat side by side on the swing. Out of habit, Sophie began to push the swing back and forth. The creaking of the chain, a memory from her youth, vied with the croaking of bullfrogs and the singing of crickets, creating a soothing ambience they both needed desperately.

"Reed told me what happened when Granddad met with Mr. Hardisty," Cassidy said at last, slanting a glance at Sophie. "He said he didn't know about me until I came to his office today. Do you believe him?"

"I do," Sophie said, nodding. "After we compared notes, I think it's pretty clear we were both lied to about what went on between our fathers."

"He said Granddad Delaney beat you when he found out you were pregnant. He didn't really...*beat* you did he?"

Sophie closed her eyes and shook her head in denial of Cassidy's question. She didn't even want to think about any of this, but maybe the past was like a festering boil. Maybe it should be lanced open by the truth so that all the ugliness and poison could ooze out and true healing begin.

"He hit me with his fists, Cassidy. On the body. He never left marks—at least not on me and Mama— where anyone could see them. I had a cracked rib from when he first found out I was pregnant. The night I refused to get an abortion, he hit me in the stomach. He wanted me to miscarry."

Cassidy's eyes, already swimming with tears, grew wide in horror. "Oh, Mom!"

Sophie wondered how her sweet and—until now—relatively innocent child would handle the ugly truth of her family.

"Reed told me the truth about Uncle Donovan and Granddad, too."

Sophie's stunned gaze flew to Cassidy's. How could he know the truth? No one knew but her and Donovan and God.

"I guess you never told me the real reason Uncle Donovan shot Granddad, because you didn't want me to know he'd abused you."

Sophie could only nod and stare at her daughter in relief.

"If Granddad Delaney did what you said he did, then it seems to me Uncle Donovan was only protecting himself and you."

"I think that's the way the courts saw it, Cassidy," Sophie said, choosing her words carefully. "Self-defense."

Cassidy sat quietly for a moment. "If the story Mr. Hardisty told Reed is so different from what Granddad told you, how do you know who's telling the truth?"

"We don't," Sophie said. "And, I'm not sure it matters. They both lied and for self-serving reasons. The main thing is that we've gotten past it."

They swung in silence for long moments, listening to the night sounds and letting the cool evening breeze ease their weary minds.

"What now?" Cassidy asked at last.

"What do you mean?"

"I mean, what happens now that I know. What happens with me and…Reed."

Sophie had no idea how to answer. "I don't know that anything will happen—or change."

"He told me he's glad we both had Dad and that he doesn't want to take his place, but he does want to make a place for himself in my life."

A pang, not unlike jealousy, pierced Sophie's heart. Cassidy had been all hers since Jake died, and she wasn't sure she wanted the status quo changed. On the other hand, she knew that even if Reed and Cassidy never formed an amicable relationship, they deserved the chance to try, especially since it wasn't Reed's fault they'd been denied a familial connection.

"How do you feel about that?"

"I guess it's okay." Cassidy looked at her questioningly. "What about you and Reed?"

"Me?" Sophie asked.

"Yeah." Cassidy met Sophie's gaze, curiously. "Did you love him when you were sixteen?"

"I thought I did, or I would never have gotten…intimate with him," Sophie confessed after a moment's careful consideration.

"What about now?"

"Now?"

Cassidy nodded. "Now. Now that all this has come out into the open, and you know you were both lied to, what now? If I see Reed on some sort of basis, you'll be part of it. Does that bother you?"

"No," Sophie said quickly.

"So if you loved him once, do you still have any feelings for him after all this time?"

Oh, she had feelings all right. But she wasn't sure exactly what they were. It felt like the beginnings of love, but she was afraid to trust it, afraid it was only the still-glowing embers of a youthful desire that would die out if given a chance to burn as hotly and fiercely as it had earlier that afternoon.

"I think he's a very attractive man," Sophie said in a prim voice. "And I think there's definitely something there. I'm just not sure what that is."

A ghost of a smile played at the corners of Cassidy's mouth. "He thinks he loves you, too, Mom."

Sophie's eyes, wide with surprise, met Cassidy's. "He does?"

"Yeah," Cassidy said with a nod. "At least, he's pretty sure it's love. He was very up front about his feelings and about his shortcomings. I think he's sorry for the way things turned out, and I think he'd like to be part of your life, too."

A tiny sprig of hope sprouted in Sophie's heart, but she knew there was one more thing she had to do before she could consider the past truly put to rest and look ahead to a possible future with Reed.

By the time ten o'clock rolled around and Cassidy, at her own suggestion, was tucked safely into bed, Sophie was emotionally drained. She found Donovan and Reed sitting outside, drinking iced tea and discussing the merits of wooden tree boxes over plastic.

They looked up when she stepped out on the porch, and Donovan scooted over so she could join him on the swing. "I want to tell Reed the truth," she said without giving him any warning.

"Sophe," Donovan warned in a sharp voice. "We agreed."

It didn't surprise her that he knew instantly what she was talking about. "I know we did, but today has taught me that nothing much good comes from lies. Just look at you."

"I'm fine," he bit out. "Better than fine."

"I have to do this, Donovan. I can never have a future with Reed until I'm totally honest with him— assuming he wants to have a future with me."

Reed, who was listening with avid interest and clearly wondering what they were talking about, smiled, reached for her hand and said, "He sure wants to give it a shot."

"Don't do this, Sophe," Donovan said, rising and going to the far end of the porch that ran the width of the house.

"I've already called Sheriff Lawrence. He said he'd be here in a few minutes."

Donovan's curse blistered the night. "Telling won't change anything. It won't turn back time."

"No, but it might give us both a clear future."

Looking as if he'd like to throttle her, Donovan swore again, then stomped down the steps and disappeared into the blackness of the night.

"What's going on?" Reed asked.

Sophie gave his hand a squeeze then dropped it. "You'll find out soon enough." Lights flickered through the copse of trees. "There's Sheriff Lawrence now."

In a matter of minutes Micah Lawrence had pulled the county vehicle to a stop and unfolded his lanky, six-foot, four-inch frame from the interior.

"Evenin' Sophie…Reed," the still attractive, white-haired sheriff said, doffing his hat and sauntering up onto the porch.

"Hello, Sheriff," Sophie replied, scooting the rocker forward. "Have a seat."

Reed gave a single nod. "Sheriff."

Micah Lawrence settled himself into the chair,

pinned Sophie with a curious look and asked, "What can I do for you, Sophie?"

"I called you because a lot of lies have been told over the years, and a lot of people have suffered unnecessarily. I mean to put an end to it." She took a deep breath. "I called you out here to confess to my father's shooting."

"What?" Reed said.

Sophie held out a hand. "Don't judge me yet. Just listen." She turned to Micah Lawrence. "Despite what you heard before, this is the way it really happened. I was washing dishes when Dad came home...."

Sophie's hands moved slowly through the soapy water, one arm pressed against her aching rib, her mind on automatic pilot as she relived every detail of the night she'd lost her virginity to Reed and he'd left her at the end of the lane. She was so wrapped up in her thoughts she didn't hear her dad's truck coming up the lane and had no idea Hutch had returned until the back door crashed against the wall and he stumbled into the room that did double duty as both kitchen and dining room.

Donovan hadn't come in from work yet, and her mother had gone to visit a sick friend, leaving the liver and onions she'd fixed earlier in the oven and Sophie to clean up the mess. Where Hutch Delaney had been that evening was anyone's guess. But now that he'd returned, Sophie knew from the degree of his drunkenness that things had either gone well...or they hadn't. Success or failure—either was reason enough for Hutch to tie one on.

She took one look at him and dreaded what was to

come—dinner was too dry or too hot or not what he wanted; where the hell had Ruby gone, anyway? Sophie didn't even bother to turn around when he shuffled into the kitchen.

"Come 'ere and lookit what I got for ya, girl," Hutch said in a whisky-thickened voice.

Seldom a nice man since the accident, he grew even meaner when he was drunk, a nightly occurrence. Knowing there was no way she could ignore a direct command, Sophie reached for the ragged dish towel, obeying the order but in no hurry as she moved toward the table. Her ribs still pained her unbearably if she moved too fast. Hutch stood on the far side of the pine dining table that sat in front of a huge rock fireplace. When she lowered her gaze and saw what he was talking about, she gasped in surprise. Hundred-dollar bills—more money than she'd seen in her sixteen years—lay fanned out over the table's scarred top. Hutch beamed at her, clearly proud of himself.

"Where did you get that?" she asked in a shocked whisper.

"Rowland Hardisty. Issa little goin'-away present for you."

A chill swept through her. "You went to see Rowland Hardisty?"

"Damn straight I did," Hutch said, hitching up his double-knit, Western-style slacks. "Was his boy knocked you up, wuddn' it?"

Sophie winced at the coarse wording. Of its own volition, one hand moved to her stomach, the other to the scabbed cut riding the crest of her right cheek. Somehow, getting knocked up sounded far worse than getting in trouble, or having a baby out of wedlock.

"Well," Hutch bellowed when she didn't answer. "Wuddn' it?"

She raised eyes that held the barest hint of anger to her father's. "Yes," she said, quickly masking her feelings with the calm face she tried so hard to adopt whenever he was around.

"Well, all right then," Hutch said with a coarse laugh. "I took care of things for you. I called Hardisty at his house bright an' early this morning and told him what was up. Met him out at that Grayson fellow's cabin tonight an' tol' him I thought his boy ought to do the right thing by you."

Sophie's heart sank. *A little going-away present from Rowland Hardisty.* Even though she'd known she had little choice, Sophie hadn't wanted to tell Reed about the baby any more than she'd wanted her father to find out. She knew her reluctance was rooted in her fear of Reed's reaction to the news after the way they'd parted.

"He said he unnerstood how this could have happened, you being such a pretty thing and all, but that his boy was too young to settle down. He's still got college to finish an' law school after that."

So you get a little going-away present, Sophie.

"An' since you're nothin' but a baby yourself, he figured the most sensible thing to do would be for you to go out of town and get an abortion. That's why he gave me the money, Sophie, so you can get rid of the baby and start over somewhere. Get a second chance."

"No."

He must have not heard her, because he smiled, a slick smile that turned her stomach. "'Course, I'll take a cut of it, since I was the one who negotiated for it and all, but—''

''I said no.'' Sophie was shocked at the determination she heard in her voice. This time it silenced Hutch.

He rounded the table, his fake ostrich-skin boots thudding on the pine floor, the look in his eyes one that would curdle the Devil's insides. ''What'd you say?''

''I'm not having an abortion. I—''

Whatever she was about to say was cut off by the blow that sent her sprawling onto the floor. Already bruised—possibly cracked—ribs, responded with a sickening surge of pain. She lifted her right hand to her cheek and felt the sticky warmth of blood. He'd reopened the cut that was just starting to heal.

''You know better than to talk back to me, missy,'' he said, grabbing her shoulders and hauling her to her feet. Rage made him oblivious to her pain, not that he'd have been sympathetic if he had noticed.

He let her go, and Sophie swayed on her feet, sinking her teeth into her lower lip as she struggled against the waves of nausea and dizziness that threatened to tow her under. She knew him well enough to know it wasn't over yet.

''You'll damn well do as I say.''

''I won't have an abortion.'' Sophie voiced her defiance through teeth clenched against the fiery pain.

''Then we'll get rid of it some other way.''

There was a new ugliness in his voice. She forced her tear-glazed eyes open in time to see him pull back his fist. Instinct made her pivot away, but not in time to completely dodge the blow that landed on her hip. She stumbled another few feet, hitting her shin on the hearth and scrabbling at the rock fireplace to keep from falling. Something thudded to the floor behind her.

Risking a glance over her shoulder, she saw Hutch lying facedown, where the momentum of his swing had carried him. With his blacker-than-Hades eyes burning with anger and cursing her with every breath, Hutch pushed himself to his feet. "I'll kill you."

Sophie felt a fresh spurt of panic. The look in his eyes said he meant it. "Please," she choked, uncertain if the word was a plea to her father to stop, or a supplication to God to intervene. "Please." As she uttered the petition, she turned away, searching for a route of escape, searching…and lifted her gaze upward. The twelve-gauge shotgun rested in a rack over the mantel, ready to take vengeance on the armadillos that ravaged the yard and the occasional skunk that wandered too close to the house. Sophie knew it was loaded. So did her father….

"I thought I could put enough fear into him, make him leave me alone until Mama got home and could talk some sense into him," she said as tears streamed down her cheeks.

Micah Lawrence didn't say a word. He rocked and listened.

As she'd recounted her tale, Donovan had returned and lowered himself to the steps. He sat there, his elbows propped on his knees, his head in his hands. Occasionally he'd give his head a slow shake as if he couldn't believe she was doing what she was. "Stop, Sis," he said now. "You don't have to say anything else."

"No. I want to tell it. I can't live with the guilt

anymore.'' She took the fresh hanky the sheriff offered and wiped at her eyes, then told how she'd
forced herself to ignore the pain in her side as she
raised her arms and took down the shotgun....

"Stay away from me," she warned, crying so hard
from pain and fear that her father was nothing but a
blurry form swaying before her.

"Or what?" Hutch snarled. "You gonna shoot
me?" He laughed, a harsh, unpleasant sound. "I don't
think so. But when I take that damned shotgun away
from you, you'll rue the day you ever thought you
could sass your old dad."

He took a step toward her. Another. The burden of
the gun weighed heavily on her trembling arms.
"Please stop!" she screamed as he took another step.

He reached out to wrest the firearm away from her
and, with a sob, Sophie squeezed her eyes shut and
shook her head in denial. A thunderous noise rever-
berated throughout the room. When she opened her
eyes, she fully expected to see Hutch standing there,
his thin lips curved in his familiar, evil smile.

Instead, he lay on the floor, his throat and shirtfront
covered with blood. Before she grasped the fact that
she'd actually pulled the trigger, she heard footsteps
pounding on the back porch....

"It was Donovan. He took one look at Dad and
started telling me what we'd tell the law when they
got there. At first I didn't understand what he was
getting at. When I realized he meant to take the
blame, I tried to argue with him, but he wouldn't
listen. He kept saying I couldn't go to jail, that I

couldn't survive if I did. That I had to think about the baby.

"He thought that since everyone knew Dad had beaten both of us up pretty good less than a week before, it would be self-defense. But then, of course, someone remembered hearing Donovan say that if Dad ever touched either of us again, he'd kill him. The lawyers did their usual dealmaking, and he wound up doing some time."

The corners of her mouth turned up in a humorless smile. "Neither of us was thinking too straight or we'd have realized that if *I'd* taken the blame it probably would have been considered justifiable homicide."

No one spoke for long moments. Only the creaking of the rocker and the sounds of the night intruded on the silence stretching among the quartet on the porch.

Reed's stomach churned, and he felt hot tears sting his own eyes. He'd heard the rumors about Hutch Delaney's abuse of his family as he'd grown up, but it hadn't had any impact on him. Things like that were far removed from his life, and there was always speculation about that kind of thing in a small town. By the time he'd read the newspaper accounts of the trial, he'd been married to Lara and so wrapped up in his own misery—not to mention being furious over Sophie marrying Jake—that he hadn't given thought to anything but his own bitter feelings.

Now, thinking of Sophie taking blows from Hutch's ham-like fists because of him—to save his baby—Reed wanted to crawl in a hole. Wanted to die. But life wasn't that kind. It was a burden he'd have to carry to his grave. No wonder she resented him.

Sophie cleared her throat and broke the stillness.

''I thought you should know the truth so that Donovan's name can be cleared. He's given up part of his life for me. Now he wants to start over here, and people should know he's innocent.''

''I'm a big boy, little sister,'' Donovan snarled, leaping to his feet. ''I don't need you to try to make things right. You're just spilling your guts to get rid of your own guilt, to make yourself feel better.''

''And I do!'' she cried.

''What's Reed have to do with all this?'' the sheriff asked, speaking for the first time and cocking his head in Reed's direction.

''My daughter is his child,'' Sophie said, with a lift of her chin. Twisting her hands in her lap, she explained that the whole thing had come to a head that morning when Cassidy had overheard her and Donovan talking, and how she and Reed had argued their way to the truth.

Reed shot a glance at the sheriff to gauge his reaction, but all the older man did was cross his legs and fold his hands over his flat stomach.

''So what happens now?'' Sophie asked. ''Do you take me in? Will I be tried?''

''For what?''

Astonishment crossed Sophie's face. ''Micah. I just told you that I was the one to pull the trigger, not Donovan.''

Micah Lawrence stuck his little finger in his ear and gave it a good shake. ''I'll be sixty next month, and to be honest with you, Sophie girl, my hearin' ain't what it used to be, if you get my drift.''

''But I—''

He plopped his hat onto his thick white hair. ''My personal feeling is that your daddy got what he deserved. As a professional lawman, I feel the shooter paid his debt to society. My daddy used to say 'Let sleeping dogs lie.' I don't see no sense openin' up a can of worms when it looks like things are goin' along pretty well for the two of you."

He got to his feet and tipped his hat to Sophie. "You and your girl have a safe trip back to Louisiana, now, hear?"

He extended a hand to Donovan. "I've been wantin' to do something with the backyard. You might want to stop by and take a look."

"Yes, sir," Donovan said. "I'll do that."

Micah turned to Reed. "See you at Rotary on Tuesday. G'night, now."

Dumbfounded, not only by Sophie's confession, but by the sheriff's willingness to look the other way, Reed could only nod and watch as the older man got into his car and drove away. Micah Lawrence was known for his hard stand on crime, as well as for following the book. He was also known for his tender heart.

Reed and the others watched the patrol car's lights disappear down the lane. Then Donovan turned and pulled his sister into a loose embrace. "Crazy woman."

"He isn't going to do anything," Sophie said in amazement.

"It's like he said," Reed told them, speaking for the first time since the sheriff had arrived. "Donovan paid for whatever happened. What's the sense in making you pay, too?"

"Exactly," Donovan said. He held Sophie at arm's length. "I hope you aren't planning on telling Cassidy."

Sophie glanced at Reed. "No," she said softly. "There's no sense causing her any more grief."

"Thank God." Donovan turned her around and gave her a little push toward Reed. "She's a hard woman to deal with. Stubborn as all get-out and very opinionated. It'd be a relief if you took her off my hands."

"Donovan!" Sophie chided, glancing at Reed with a look akin to horror.

Reed gave a half smile. "I can see that, and we'll work on it."

Donovan brushed a kiss to Sophie's cheek and went inside, leaving Sophie alone with Reed, her heart beating in time to the cricket's call. Their eyes met, and an awkward tension built between them. Sophie crossed her arms over her breasts in a nervous gesture.

"I hope you don't let any of this color your relationship with Cassidy. And I hope this is one secret the three of us can keep."

"I won't be saying anything to her," Reed said. "I never did find much sport in pulling wings off butterflies."

"Thank you." Unable to bear his intense scrutiny, she turned her back on him, clutched the porch railing and leaned out over the bed of peonies and thrift blooming there.

Maybe…if there was a God in heaven, Reed wouldn't hate her for what she'd done. If she couldn't have his love, maybe she could at least have his forgiveness. "I suppose you're shocked and horrified."

"Yes."

Reed's admission carried to her on the nighttime

breeze. Sophie closed her eyes and held on tighter, bidding goodbye to the last of her dreams.

"But not by what you said or did," Reed continued. She heard his footfalls on the worn wooden porch, felt his body brush hers as he moved to stand behind her. Close behind her. She held her breath, afraid to hear what he might say, afraid not to.

"I'm shocked at how you had to live. Horrified at the thought of anyone having to put up with what you and your brother and mother did. And I'm amazed that you both came out of it so normal and well-adjusted."

The breath Sophie wasn't even aware she was holding soughed from her lips in a soft sigh. She dropped her head and fought the urge to cry again, even as she wondered how there could possibly be any tears left inside her.

"I always knew you were strong," he said slipping his arms around her and folding his hands over her abdomen.

She resisted for a moment, then gave in to the urging of her heart and let her body go lax against his.

"I think that's one of the things about you that impressed me the most. But it scared me, too."

She glanced over her shoulder at him. "Scared you? Why?"

"It would have been so easy to lean on that strength, and I know now that if I had, I'd never have been able to really break away from my father. God knows it's been hard enough."

"I didn't feel strong," she said in a tremulous voice. "The only time I wasn't scared was when Donovan was at home. I knew he'd protect me from Daddy as much as he could, or die trying. And the night my father found out I was pregnant, I thought he would."

Reed held her tighter. "Did it happen often?"

"He didn't hit me often," Sophie said, "and when he did, never where anyone could see that he had. But he seemed to like beating Donovan down." Her smile was more bitter than sweet. "Everyone in town thought Donovan stayed banged up because he was a brawler."

"I know," Reed concurred. "All us city boys wanted to stay clear of him."

"It was so unfair of me to expect him to protect me," she said, talking into his shirtfront. "He took his first blow for me when he was only nine."

Reed's stomach clutched. He wondered again how Donovan Delaney managed to come out of such a background so happy and well-adjusted.

Sophie tipped back her head to look up at him. "He gave up part of his life for me."

"And you were willing to give it back."

A sob worked its way free, and the next thing he knew, she was crying and clinging to him again. A feeling of déjà vu swept over him along with a rising desire. There'd be no lovemaking this time, though. Not with Cassidy and Donovan in the house.

"What's going to happen now?" she asked, when she got her tears under control.

"We're going to give ourselves a chance."

"You mean you want us to...to have an affair?"

"I never was much good at those," Reed said. "But I do like being married."

She gasped. "Surely you aren't proposing."

"No. Not yet. But it's something I want us to consider." He kissed her eyelids and the corners of her mouth. "I want us to start with where we are right now. I want to date you. To get to know you. I want you to get to know me. Let's see where it leads. If we don't make it, at least we'll know we gave it our best shot.

"I never forgot you, Sophie. Never. You've been with me these past seventeen years more than it's comfortable for me to admit, especially since I was married to another woman for most of that time."

Ruby Delaney used to say that all things happen for a reason. Sophie had been quick to use the fact that she and Reed weren't the same people they'd been as kids to negate the possibility of their finding any happiness together. But growing older and wiser, becoming more independent and sure of oneself wasn't bad. Neither was having opinions or breaking out of the mold.

She considered the possibility that she and Reed had been separated to give him the time he needed to grow up, to find himself, to become a man strong enough to stand up to his father. And that she'd been given the chance to grow into the kind of woman a man like Reed needed at his side. Yes, they'd changed, but suddenly she saw those changes as good things. The test was to see if they liked the people they'd become. So far she was very impressed in the changes she saw in Reed.

For the first time in a long time, she felt hope. She saw the determination in his eyes that matched the tenacity in her heart. "We'll make it," she said firmly.

"I think you're right," he said, brushing her hair away from her face with a gentle hand.

He kissed her then, and for long moments there was

no doubt in either of their minds that their declarations were true. Finally, when Reed let her breath again, she asked, "What about my practice?"

He nuzzled her ear, breathing in the delicious scent of her. "Not a problem. People move businesses all the time, and Lewiston could probably use a good family counselor." He kissed her, and his hands started moving over her body as if he wanted to memorize every curve and hollow.

Moments later she started with her objections again. "Your dad—"

"Can take a flying leap."

"Lara—"

"Is the one who told me to go after you."

"Really?" Sophie said.

"Really."

"Donovan—"

"Can darn well find his own woman," Reed said, lowering his head to claim her lips.

Sophie smiled against his mouth. "I think he has someone in mind."

That got Reed's attention. He cocked a quizzical eyebrow. "No kidding! Who?"

"Your ex-wife."

"Lara?" Reed said, clearly stunned. "You've got to be kidding."

"Nope." While she waited for him to come to grips with the news she'd just delivered, she said, "So we're really going to do this—give it a try?"

"What? Oh, yes," he said, sliding his hands to her hips and pulling her against him. "We're definitely going to give it a try."

Later, after Reed left the house, albeit reluctantly, he thought about what Sophie had told him. Lara and

Donovan. Another missing piece of the puzzle fell into place. Sophie's statement left no doubt that Donovan Delaney was the father of the baby Lara had carried for such a short time.

Donovan and Lara.

Who'd have ever guessed?

* * * * *

*If Reed and Sophie have finally
found happiness, can there
be hope for Lara and Donovan?*

Find out next month in

LARA'S LOVER—

*coming in December 2000,
only from Silhouette Special Edition.*

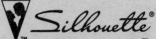

You're not going to believe this offer!

In October and November 2000, buy any two Harlequin or Silhouette books and save $10.00 off future purchases, or buy any three and save $20.00 off future purchases!

Just fill out this form and attach 2 proofs of purchase (cash register receipts) from October and November 2000 books and Harlequin will send you a coupon booklet worth a total savings of $10.00 off future purchases of Harlequin and Silhouette books in 2001. Send us 3 proofs of purchase and we will send you a coupon booklet worth a total savings of $20.00 off future purchases.

Saving money has never been this easy.

I accept your offer! Please send me a coupon booklet:

Name: _____

Address: _____ City: _____

State/Prov.: _____ Zip/Postal Code: _____

Optional Survey!

In a typical month, how many Harlequin or Silhouette books would you buy <u>new</u> at retail stores?

☐ Less than 1 ☐ 1 ☐ 2 ☐ 3 to 4 ☐ 5+

Which of the following statements best describes how you <u>buy</u> Harlequin or Silhouette books? Choose one answer only that <u>best</u> describes you.

☐ I am a regular buyer and reader
☐ I am a regular reader but buy only occasionally
☐ I only buy and read for specific times of the year, e.g. vacations
☐ I subscribe through Reader Service but also buy at retail stores
☐ I mainly borrow and buy only occasionally
☐ I am an occasional buyer and reader

Which of the following statements best describes how you <u>choose</u> the Harlequin and Silhouette series books you buy <u>new</u> at retail stores? By "series," we mean books within a particular line, such as *Harlequin PRESENTS* or *Silhouette SPECIAL EDITION.* Choose one answer only that <u>best</u> describes you.

☐ I only buy books from my favorite series
☐ I generally buy books from my favorite series but also buy books from other series on occasion
☐ I buy some books from my favorite series but also buy from many other series regularly
☐ I buy all types of books depending on my mood and what I find interesting and have no favorite series

Please send this form, along with your cash register receipts as proofs of purchase, to:
In the U.S.: Harlequin Books, P.O. Box 9057, Buffalo, NY 14269
In Canada: Harlequin Books, P.O. Box 622, Fort Erie, Ontario L2A 5X3
(Allow 4-6 weeks for delivery) Offer expires December 31, 2000.

PHQ4002

Silhouette®

where love comes alive—online...

eHARLEQUIN.com

your romantic life

—Romance 101—
♥ Guides to romance, dating and flirting.

—Dr. Romance—
♥ Get romance advice and tips from
our expert, Dr. Romance.

—Recipes for Romance—
♥ How to plan romantic meals for you
and your sweetie.

—Daily Love Dose—
♥ Tips on how to keep the romance
alive every day.

—Tales from the Heart—
♥ Discuss romantic dilemmas with other
members in our Tales from the Heart
message board.

If you enjoyed what you just read,
then we've got an offer you can't resist!

Take 2 bestselling love stories FREE!

Plus get a FREE surprise gift!

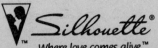

#1 *New York Times* bestselling author

NORA ROBERTS

introduces the loyal and loving, tempestuous and
tantalizing Stanislaski family.

Coming in November 2000:

The Stanislaski Brothers
Mikhail and Alex

Their immigrant roots and warm, supportive home had
made Mikhail and Alex Stanislaski both strong and
passionate. And their charm makes them irresistible....

In February 2001, watch for
THE STANISLASKI SISTERS: *Natasha and Rachel*

And a brand-new Stanislaski story from Silhouette Special Edition,
CONSIDERING KATE

Available at your favorite retail outlet.

Silhouette®
Where love comes alive™

Visit Silhouette at www.eHarlequin.com   PSSTANBR2